SCANDALOUS

Billie Dureya Shell

SCANDALOUS

Copyright © 2020

All rights reserved to Billie Dureyea Shell.

No part of this publication may be reproduced, distributed or transmitted in any form or by any means, including photocopying, or other electronic or mechanical methods, without the prior written permission of the publisher, except in the case of brief quotations embodied in critical reviews and certain noncommercial uses permitted by copyright law. Any references to historical events, real people or real places are used factiously. Names, characters, and places are products of the authors imagination.

Front Cover Image By grafic designer Billie Dureyea Shell & Kenny Writes

First Printing Edition 2020

ISBN 978-0-578-68155-9

This book is dedicated to:

To my mom & Daughter Alura I love you this
one is 4 you.......

Team Shell

Acknowledgement

—————— ✦ ——————

Once again I want 2 give thank 2 God for this gift I am so grateful for him giving me away 2 provide 4 my family in my house we will alwayz put you first.

To my mother Mclessie Shell you taught me so much and you loved me NO MATTER WHAT I love you so much momma.... What's up on with some bake chicken LOL☺.

To my little sister Glenda I love you and miss you blackie get at ur big brother Lil Sis.

To my Wife Shatoya Shell you get on my damn nerves but I wouldnt trade you 4 anything. In the world I love you more then words can ever express.

To all my children I love y'all Jazmine, Ant'Tuan, Davon, Anthony, David, Lil Dureyea, Alura, Queen Diavion, Cameron, Preniece, Shaniece and Tajh I love u all and I'll 4ever have ur back you all give me a reason 2 smile.......... to my cousin Zane RIP nigga I miss u more then anyone will ever no, your always remembered love you bro.

To my cousin. Ty I miss you thank 4 looking out 4 me and Zane you played a big part in my life and I always looked up to you l love you... Uncle Woody I miss you and love you, you no your my favorite uncle....

To my nigga Jamal love you, my brothers Lawrence and fred thank 4 showing me the game I love yall 4 that.

To my old est sister Nedra love you thank you 4 always having my back. to my family uncles anties cousins etc.. I love y'all even those of you that act funny as fuck

To my dark side niggas y'all no what it is YAAH GANG........

Now to all my readers and fans I love you thanks for reading I hope u enjoy this book as much as I enjoy writing them with this Corona Virus 19 shit there ain't shit to do but write so I'm on my shit with that being said y'all be safe cover your face and love each other life is short so love the ones that really love you I'm gone enjoy the book

Billie Dureyea Shell

"I think I am going to do it," Donesha said, suddenly sitting up on the therapist's couch—back straight and head up—she was so sure. "What is that...what will you do?" her therapist asked, waiting for Donesha to say the words they had worked toward for over a year. "I am finally going to tell my mom that... that I was molested." Donesha let out a full breath of air and slumped back onto the couch. "When she asks you by who...will you tell her?" She nodded yes, thinking back to that day at her grandmother's house. How she thought it was a game, just what kids did. Until she got older, years crept past and she felt different when he was around—a weird tingling in her stomach that made her feel angry. When she was thirteen, she'd put the pieces together but pushed the thoughts to the side. But now, after a year, she was able to say "molested" and her name in the same sentence. Now she was ready to say it out loud. "She'll probably know already that it was something at my granny's house." Donesha chuckled a bit at the thought. "I can't believe I'm here telling you all of this. I never dreamed that I would be able to talk this freely." It was an empowering moment, looking back over how far she had come since she put the jigsaw puzzle pieces of her memory back together. "Now remember what we talked about, right?" Ms. Palmer the therapist said. "However she reacts has…" "Nothing to do with me…it is from her own reality and perspective." "Exactly." Ms. Palmer was pleased, wishing that she could hug her client after all of the progress she had made. "Great. Our time is up. I'll see you in two weeks and you can tell me how everything went." They shook hands, an eager Donesha smiling from ear to ear, happy for someone to listen and be on her side. "Sounds good. See you then."

Dr. Palmer watched as Donesha bounced from the room, through the lobby and out the door into the cold Chicago air. Leaving the small campus counseling center, Donesha smiled thinking about the winter break. Usually going back home meant a slew of emotions but today she was ready. "C'mon let's go." her twin yelled from the car. Hopping in the passenger side, the car eased away from the curb before she got her seat belt on. "I'm going to do it. I talked to her and I think I'm going to do it now," she said, just as sure now as she had been in the office. "Cool Sis...I'm with you. But do you think it matters?" The glare that Donesha shot at her sister could have killed a few dozen men. "Hell yeah, it matters. She was away at work when all that shit went on. You know how Grandma used to treat me." "I wasn't there all the time, remember. I don't know." "Ohhh yeah, that's right. You were off playing pianos and catching fireflies at music camps." Lanesha rolled her eyes at her sister's smart-ass comment and refocused her eyes back to the road. "Whatever, Nene...I didn't mean it like that. I'm just saying." "Yeah I'm just saying some shit to. I'm telling Mama—finally"

They sat with quiet between them, just the sound of Lanesha's tires speeding up on the highway pavement. "So how are you going to say it?" Lanesha finally asked. "I got five hours till we get home to think about it." Home for the holidays brought the usual fakeness. Hugs, smiles, and promises that would never happen. But this year Donesha promised herself she was going to open her mouth and talk for once. It was hard finding the proper time. Once they got home, the girls were swept away on random shopping trips, store runs, and taste-testings. But on Christmas Eve, Donesha finally found a time to catch her mother alone. Late at night on the enclosed back porch, as her mother checked the meat smoker— Donesha went for it. Stepping out onto the porch sent her heart pounding like a drum. Yvette, her mother, barely looked up when she came out onto the porch. Her hair was wrapped up tight as a beehive while she shifted racks and checked the meat. "Ma...can I talk to you?" "Sure boo...you came out here to help?" She asked laughing. "Nah...not really. I just...I wanted to tell you about some stuff." She relayed the situation word for word like her therapist taught her—starting off slowly, with the time and specific situations so her mother would remember. "Remember when Lanesha got that piano camp scholarship and you were working out of town, and I had to stay by myself with Grandma?" "Yeah...I remember..." "Grandma...she wasn't that nice to me." Donesha thought about the nights being awakened from her bed to go rewash a cabinet full of clean dishes. Or being made to sit in the house all summer because someone called the house after eight p.m. "Oh girl...you know Mama is a damn firecracker." Yvette said not even bother to look her daughter's way as she swatted down her complaints. "I know that, but it wasn't about her being a firecracker. She was really bad to me and I don't want to be around her tomorrow." Slowly, Yvette's head crept up from the iron smoker. "You're not going with us?" "No...I don't want to go in her house ever again." "Why? What did she do that was so bad to you..." "She let me get molested." The words just fell out of her mouth. She didn't plan it, but there they were out in the open. "She what?" Donesha went over everything in as much detail as she could. "Mr. Clarkson...he was drunk." "Her boyfriend—Mr. Clarkson?" Donesha nodded, thinking hard on that night. The story had never changed for her, and the therapist had said as the years went on, the thoughts and memories of that night would get more and more vivid. "I screamed—I called for granny and she didn't come. The next day she told me not to tell anybody. Not even you." By now Donesha was bawling, her tears heavily streaming down her face in a flood. "Mama, I still think about it. I told myself it didn't happen but it did...it did." By now, a normal mother would have wrapped her arms around her daughter—and comforted her until the tears stopped—but not Yvette. Instead, she smoked a long Virginia Slim, gawking at her daughter as if she were some sort of alien. "Save all the crying shit, Donesha. You know you was fast girl." Yvette laughed taking a long drag of her cigarette and blowing it into Donesha's face. "Wha...what? He touched me...he made me do things... he told me not to tell." Donesha was baring her soul, something she rarely did—especially with her mother—

but her words did nothing to penetrate Yvette's cold heart. "Your granny told me about your fast ass trying to fuck with Mr. Dennison's grandson. So don't tell me shit about that. You brought it on yourself." Donesha felt like dust, dirt on the floor, or even lower than that if it were possible. "No I didn't...I'm telling you what happened. After all this time..." She tried reasoning and giving valid rebuttals that she learned in therapy, but not even a year of therapy would prepare her for the reaction of Yvette Hollins. "Look baby, I'm sorry that happened to you, okay? But you got to remember to keep your legs closed and stay away from boys and men like that. You gotta be responsible. " In a few seconds ,Yvette was able to undo what had taken a year's worth of counseling to build. "Hell, it's up to you to hear what a man is thinking. If you were too slow to get out of there, then..." Yvette shrugged her shoulders, blowing cigarette smoke into her daughter's face. "Now what's really bothering you? Maybe it's the stress from school. But don't go on and on about that molesting shit, you hear me? Mama would have a fucking stroke if she heard you talk like that and…" Before Yvette could finish her sentence, a chime from the doorbell broke up their thoughts. "Shit, that's him. He's early." Yvette scrambled into the house toward the front door. Donesha walked behind her wiping her tears with her sleeve as her mother did what she did best, and that was ignore her needs. I hate this bitch, she told herself, as she followed behind Yvette. She eyed the knives on the kitchen counter. She envisioned herself taking the biggest one and jamming it into her mother's throat for not believing her. Then she would take the same knife, drive to her grandmother's, and do the same thing. Dumb bitches. Fuck them, she told herself as Yvette answered the door. "Hey Clarence. You're a little early aren't you?" She had never seen the man before. He was probably another entrant into her mother's revolving door of men. "Hey baby…" He came through the door hugging Yvette close but over her shoulder, his eyes were on Donehsa. She looked back for a moment, gazing at the hazel eyes of the man her mother was embracing. Then she noticed his arms, Donesha had a personal fetish with biceps and this creature had a perfect set, as well as pectoral muscles for her to press on. "Oh... Clarence...I'm sorry, this is my daughter," Yvette said, turning to introduce Clarence to her firstborn. But Clarence had already fondled her with his eyes, looking over every inch of the supple body of the twenty-year-old. "Nice to meet you," Donesha said, showing her teeth with an eager smile as she extended her hand to the new, handsome older friend of her mother. "The pleasure is all mine..." He kissed her hand like in the movies, planting a peck on her skin that sent chills through her body. "Alright...come on back here, I got us some wine," Yvette said, slamming the door and pulling her new man toward the kitchen. As Yvette talked and pulled, Clarence's eyes were still all over Donesha. She was used to it. Being so beautiful and developing early, always made Donesha a target for unwanted attention. But tonight she wasn't annoyed or eager to tell her mother like usual about unwanted advances. After the conversation tonight she was done telling her mother about anything. You don't want to listen to my words...So I'm gonna show your ass better than I can tell you,

Donesha reasoned, as Clarence and Yvette disappeared into the kitchen. The talking and laughing continued, as corks popped and glasses clinked. "Psst...Psst..." Donesha swung around to see her sister in their bedroom doorway, waving her over. "Come here..." Slipping into their room, she lied down on the twin bed closest to the windows. Slumped in exhaustion, Lanesha was ready to hear all the details. "What did she say?" Lonnie asked, wishing it was a different result than their mother's nonchalant demeanor. "She told me I was fast, and that Granny had told her a different story," Donesha said to herself, thinking of the old bitch that would say anything to cover up what happened on her watch. "Are you serious? She didn't believe you at all?" Lanesha asked. "Nope, but it's all good." "What does that mean...and who is Mama is laughing with in the kitchen?" Donesha wanted to tell her, but she was too busy plotting. If her mother didn't want to believe her and would much rather believe that she was, in her opinion, "A fast-ass little girl," then so be it, Donesha thought to herself. Let the games begin.

Chapter One
DONESHA

"Ashes to ashes and dust to dust. We now lay Sister Hollins to rest. A friend, a mother, and a grandmother..." And a bitch—the pastor forgot the most important characteristic of all. That bitch would never rest, the pastor had no idea that the woman we called our grandma was cursed. She was more like the devil, but you couldn't tell our mother that. She was boo-hooing, ready to fall in the hole and die with grandma. "Mama we are going to miss you." Yvette tossed in handfuls of dirt as they lowered granny's casket into the ground. It was embarrassing, seeing her cry and throw a fit over this rotten bitch. "Why is she doing all this?" I finally leaned over, asking my twin sister. She shrugged as my mother threw in a few roses, mixing with the dirt that would surely rot my grandmother's old, decrepit soul. "I mean...it is her mother. She's allowed to grieve, Nene..." So said my twin, but I didn't agree. Nobody should be allowed to grieve for that bitch. Looking at Lanesha was like looking in the mirror, except my hair was straight, with ombre-blonde tips past my shoulders. Today, my sister's hair was shorter and naturally curly. Our hair best described our personalities—totally opposite—and that was usually how we approached life. "Yeah, I guess. I'm not doing none of that shit though," I told her, as we continued to watch. She always saw stuff that I overlooked—like some calmer version of myself. "Look at all these people. Cousins that we have never met, aunts that have been away since we were young. Yet they all run back here... for what?" "Obligation?" "No...motherfuckers love negativity. They love this shit, and you know Mama loves putting on a show." "Yeah...just like her mama..." "May God burn her soul." "Agreed." We sat on those emotions for a second, thinking about the reasons we could be happy about someone's death, when Lanesha gave me another insight. "You know that's all a show. Mama has to keep up appearances." Lanesha was like my conscience, always reminding me about shit that I forgot. Like our mother was only about what people could see, everything else was pushed to the side and had been since we played with Barbie dolls. "Fuck that bitch," I hissed, and I knew my sister felt the same way. Our grandmother was dead and we couldn't bother to try and be sad about it. As the casket continued its descent, I had a flash of my childhood. I suddenly recalled the good times when my mother was around, and the bad times when we lived with my grandmother. It was torture, and I spent a lot of time hating this woman. Now she was dead, after all those years of praying she would finally be gone. I felt like rejoicing, screaming, doing a fucking cartwheel between the tombstones—but instead I stood in the lumpy grass of the cemetery, watching as people faked tears as they walked to their cars. "I just want shit to be real. Why is our family so fake...why?" It was more of a rhetorical question, because neither I nor my sister would ever have the answer to that. "Maybe because all this shit is fake. Everybody is cheating, fucking, and stealing from somebody else in this family, so why walk around and be real when you can't look in the fucking mirror." Her words stung me in more places than I cared to admit at the moment. I knew I was doing my fair share of dirt, but I always reverted to the loner side of myself—I had to do my dirt by my lonesome. "But we just know that she's gone now. That part of our lives is officially buried and we don't have to feel obligated to feel like her step-grandchildren anymore." It was some sad shit to say, but my sister always kept it real. "Yeah, you're right sis…" Lonnie's assessment was the most accurate way to describe the bitch that birthed our mother. Growing up, she treated us like step-children at the bottom of the barrel instead of like her own flesh and blood. "You know, a big part of me feels relief, like she got what was coming to her." I could only admit these true feelings to Lanesha. Anyone else would think I was some insane psychopath—but whatever. . "Naw, she got diabetes.

What should have come to her was a bullet to the head." We laughed for a moment until Mama appeared before us. Her smeared makeup and bloodshot eyes made us straighten up like soldiers. "Girls, are you okay?" We didn't say a word, instead we looked at her like she was insane. I had enough. As the oldest, I was about to speak my mind right here in this cemetery. "Look around you… how many people do you see here?" Swiveling her head around, she joined us in taking a small survey. There were only about a dozen people at the cemetery, many of whom were running toward their cars before the pastor finished his words. "What does that have to do with anything?" Mama asked, annoyed at what already seemed like a moot point. "Everything. Nobody loved her but you. She was mean and evil to everybody else, and all these years…" "Girls, girls…let's get in the limousine. No need in having this conversation in front of everyone," Clarence said, on mama's side and defending her as usual. On the surface, he was the model husband coming to her rescue, but Mama didn't budge. Covering her hands with her ears, she took a stand.

"No...I don't want to hear any of that right now." My Mama burst out into tears. "I've told you a million times I'm sorry...I'm so sorry...I can't go back in time and fix that stuff. What else do you want from me?" She tried hugging me but I wasn't interested in having her hands on me at all. "I'm so sorry for what happened to you and I promise I will spend the rest of my life making it right." She was preaching to the choir and saying all the stereotypical things, but I knew she didn't mean them. It was a rehearsed statement with no feeling behind it, that she'd built up from years of therapy. But in reality, there was no way you can apologize to a person for putting them in a place that facilitated rape. I hated to think about it. Actually it wasn't rape, it was molestation. I was a child too young to fight him off, and my mother wasn't there. My grandmother turned a blind eye and now here we are in a cemetery arguing over the woman who allowed me to be hurt. There was no way my mother could apologize for that, and here she was pleading for my forgiveness—but I was deaf to sympathy. I was more interested in revenge. It was the only thing that people understood. I've figured out over the years that it's a universal language. Everyone understands pain, and I wanted this woman in front of me who shared the same DNA running through my veins, to feel the pain that I felt. The pain of being left with an abusive grandmother and all the toxic people that ran in and out of her house, and all of the things we were subjected to. I wanted my mother to feel pain. "There is nothing you can do now. I just want to go home...I don't want to ride in the limo either. I'll just take an Uber or something." "An Uber... from the goddamn cemetery. Girl, are you out of your mind?" She was getting irritated and I loved it. Every time I was able to piss her off, I did, and there was no greater thing that upset her than failing to keep up a picture-perfect appearance. "No, Yvette, I'm not out of my fucking mind. We just put the psycho bitch that was your mother in the ground, and you're up here crying like Jesus died." I was ready to go to war and rumble right here in the cemetery, but somebody saved her ass. "Hold on wait...wait…" Clarence stepped between us. The way I was feeling I was ready to throw her ass in the ground with Granny. Two funerals in one day sounded appropriate to me, but like always, Clarence was here to put out the fire. "I'll take her in my car," suggested my mother's husband, the six-foot-two giant with biceps the size of a steroid-filled bodybuilder—the image belying the advertising executive that he was. "I have to go back to the office anyway." He said straightening his jacket, and was looking back and forth from me to Yvette. "Come on...people are watching. Don't let your emotions get the best of you." Yvette breathed fire. I knew on so many levels I had pissed her off but I was done holding my tongue about Granny. She was a mean bitch, and because of my mother Yvette, I spent a lot of time with that mean bitch. I wasn't going to pretend I was distraught that she was burning in Hell. Especially after the shit that went on in that house. "That's if you can be in the same car with me for fifteen minutes." I rolled my eyes at Clarence's statement. He always said assholic shit to me that got him either cursed out or completely ignored. As angry as my mother was at me, I ceased to exist when a man was involved. She no longer cared about our argument—she was now focused on her husband. "But we have people coming to the house." She pouted, damn near poking her lip out toward Clarence like a toddler. "We talked about this, Yvette, Clarence said. This is why I drove my own car; I told you I have to wrap up this deal, then I'm all yours for the holidays. I can drop Donesha off on the way." I stood my ground, and watching my mother be disappointed about her husband not placating her with every move, made me do internal cartwheels. That's what you get bitch. Feel the fucking pain, it's nothing compared to what I feel. "Fine." She said, giving him a hug. Then she turned to me, trying to muster a smile. "I know you're angry and I'm sorry for all of that." She said it a million times, but I never believed her. She was just reciting some gibberish that sounded good. "You know...people will be asking about you." She had already moved on to what people were going to think if I wasn't at her mother's repass, but I wasn't budging. "I'd rather let Clarence take me home so I can lie down. Unless you want me to tell everyone the real stories about Granny and her house on Madison." She threw up her hands in disgust. I already knew that she wouldn't want me talking about being abused over the usual repass fixings. "Fine Donesha. Have it your way." She stormed off, walking with my sister trailing behind her to the limousine. Clarence and I watched as she smiled, shaking hands and hugging folks with politician-like precision. "I thought you wouldn't be able to pull it off." Clarence whispered as we turned and walked towards his car. "I'm not your wife, Clarence. I can do anything I want. I'm a fucking boss, not a peasant like her. That's why you want me, remember?" I whispered through gritted teeth. Walking through the uneven patches of grass in the cemetery, I felt invincible. My grandmother leaving the earth had shaken up my need for revenge. I was tired of holding in this pain, rethinking it every day of my life while my mother played the good mom and swept the shit I went through under the rug. Now walking beside me was her husband, her most prized possession, but she had no idea I had this man wrapped around my finger. "You make me so horny in that dress and the way you talk back to her. Whew... that shit makes my dick jump." He loved this shit and I knew it. He probably couldn't wait for a moment to step in and try to get me alone. I was wondering how he would do it and now he was pulling the car door open for me. "You couldn't wait could you?" I told him, seeing a sly smile part his lips. Glancing back at my mother, it was easy to see she was too busy smiling, hugging, and putting on a show to notice her man with his eyes on me. Lanesha was right beside her, kissing her ass—oblivious to it all. Meanwhile as always, my mama's men were infatuated with me, but this one was different. This time I wanted it, allowed it, encouraged it, and laughed about it. "Shhh, Mr. Jeffries. Your wife can still see us," I teased, easing into the car. "Not for long. Wait till I get your ass alone,." he said through clenched teeth as he slammed the door. He hopped in like a superhero going to fight crime and we were off, driving past my mother and sister as they hugged the family members and acted distraught. They waved and so did I, but I wanted to stick a special middle finger up at my mother as Clarence slid his hand up my thigh. "Oh, you look so fucking hot today." He was right.

I wore a dress that was especially short because Granny would have deemed it to be disrespectful. Open-toe heels way too high for church and pink sparkle nail polish on my toes completed the look, because she would have thought whores wore that. I was saying "fuck you" to a few people today, my granny, and most of all my mom, by fucking her husband. It was my best magic trick of revenge yet; revenge was the only thing that kept me sane. "I missed you...you said you were coming by my apartment last night. I almost called Mom to see where you were." I laughed as we crept out of the cemetery, with my mother so engrossed in her grief and need to feel like a victim that she didn't even notice. "You could have—she wouldn't have suspected a thing," he said, turning out of the land of tombstones and fake tears. She didn't see that her husband was obsessed with me, that every time we were together, Clarence couldn't take his eyes off me. And who was I to tell him no; I am a grown woman of twenty-five years. He isn't my father, we have no blood relation so why can't I fuck him. I explained that to myself everyday like a prayer of my innocence for what I'm doing. But as a reminder that I was wrong, my phone rings. "Shit…" "Who is it?" Clarence asked, his hand still creeping up my dress to the edge of my panties. "Tron…" my boyfriend was calling and I was letting my mother's husband fondle up my thigh. "Answer it…" he ordered. "Put it on speaker…" I did as he said, while he peeled my panties to the side. "Hello." "Hey baby…you okay?" Clarence had found my creamy center and was now strumming my clit like a guitar. His fingers were soaked, moving ever so smoothly across the swollen nub of my clit as my boyfriend's voice filled the air. "I'm sorry again that I couldn't make it. I got called in at the last second and…" "I'm fine… everything's okay." I tried to keep my voice steady as my legs did an involuntary shake from Clarence's hand. "So, you sure you okay…?" "Yes…I'm fine…I'm okay baby. I just…I'm at a loss for words right now." I was out of breath like a sprinter but nothing working harder than Clarence's fingers. He played me, strummed me, stroking my pussy like he owned it all while merging onto the highway. I wasn't sure how to feel right now so I felt nothing…

nothing but pleasure as I listened to my boyfriend and let my mother's husband's finger fuck me down the highway. All of this was a perfect combination, or a helluva storm. What could anyone expect, I was my granny's child, right? I loved drama, had an affinity for revenge, and I'm the queen at being vindictive. However bad my grandmother was, I am much worse. That's why she hated me, that's why she abused me and that's why my mother has to pay. May God burn my granny's soul.

"I just don't understand your sister—why she couldn't play nice like everyone else." It had been a week since the funeral and my mom was still blabbing on about Donesha. It was always like this, I could have been the best daughter in the world but my mother would always bring up Donesha the problem child. "Mama. It's Thanksgiving; can we leave this alone?" "Exactly...here it is Thanksgiving and she's late. She really tries my damn patience." She complained about my sister being late, but here she was still cooking last minute add-ons to the menu. In a black cocktail dress and full makeup, my mother was peeling potatoes telling me about my sister being late. None of it made sense—in our family anything rarely did—but somehow I always had to play the peacemaker. "Ma...we didn't have the best relationship with grandma. I was away at school but Donesha was at home by herself for a lot of things, so she got the brunt of that" I tried to be nice as I could and explain it, but the shit that Granny did to my sister was unforgivable, so she can't blame Donnie for not wanting to be around. "I told you girls a million times that I didn't know it was that bad. I didn't find that out until much later. But besides all that, she's dead. We can't bring her back. All we can do is be respectful." She still wasn't hearing me. She wanted us to be respectful to someone that gave the utmost disrespect. "We can't let everybody see us fall apart." That was her problem, my mother was always so worried about appearances and what everyone else thought. "Mama you gotta understand we don't care what other people thought. It can't erase the things that..." but instead of listening, she covered her ears. "No, no, no, no...not today. I don't want to hear about any of that stuff today." This was her, my mother, the person that we couldn't talk to if it was about anything with real substance. She was all about the fake stuff and smoking mirrors. "Fine, Mama, fine...you never want to listen, you just want to keep shit in the past." Before she could answer, the doorbell rang. "Oh...I gotta get the door. Hopefully that's your sister. Clarence..." "Yeah!" "People are showing up." "Okay, I'm at the door." I heard the the sounds of kids coming in, and a million hellos—then I saw him. Tron was in the middle of it all with his cocoa-brown skin and long locs, giving out hugs to my aunts, but I'm the one who wanted to be wrapped in his arms. "Oh, you're here." My sister was just a few feet in front of me, and I didn't even see her because I was so concentrated on him. "Hey!" We hugged, and I could already tell she was uneasy. "Where is Mom?" "In the kitchen. " "Good...I gotta put this food in the oven and..." A speeding toddler broke us up, running between us as the music seemed to get a few levels louder. Donesha pointed to the kitchen and I could already hear her and mom fussing. Moving toward the door, I got in the mix, giving hugs and getting cheek-kisses until I got to him. "Hey bro...what's going on?" I gave him a hug, innocent to everyone else—but to me it meant way more. My chest on his as we embraced and just close enough so I could hear, but the dozen or so people around us would have no clue. "Meet me in the garage in ten minutes," he whispered in my ear, and just as quickly as he hugged me, he let me go. But the way my heart was pounding, you would have thought he tongued me down. That's how much I loved Trontavius Pearson. The sound of my ass-clapping filled the garage. We always did it hard and fast when we were sneaking, but he was especially hard today. "It's yours, it's all yours," I told Tron, and it was the truth. The top of my head to the bottom of my pussy belonged to this man, but unfortunately all of him didn't belong to me. Still, I was like putty in his hands, or rather a quick fuck in the cold garage while my family gathered in the house for Thanksgiving dinner. But any time I had with him was stolen, so I took whatever I could get. "Yeah...toot that ass up." He lifted my dress more, grabbing onto my thong for leverage. As he pulled and I pushed, we made music with my pussy and his dick the main instrument. He was all I ever wanted and needed. We loved each other so much we couldn't keep our hands to ourselves. So at my mother's house on Thanksgiving we had no choice but to sneak away. Outside in the garage was the only place where we could be alone. Now with my dress up over my ass and my hands on my mother's car, he rammed me from behind. "Damn I missed you," he moaned as we moved together. He felt like sugar inside my pussy, a sweet treat that I couldn't get enough of. "I missed you too…" I squealed between pumps, moaning load as the wind blew snow and ice around outside. I didn't care that it was freezing. As long as Tron was with me, it was hot wherever we went. I waited for him to say he missed me too, or maybe even to tell me that he loved me, but I heard none of that. Instead he made an announcement: "I'm cumming…" and before I could make a sound, he pulled out of me and splattered his seed all over the garage floor. "What the fuck are you doing? My mom is going to see that." "Then clean it up." His dick was back in his boxers and zipped up before I could pull down my dress. Just like that, he had flipped a switch. He was back to being an asshole. "You're such an asshole. I didn't even cum. Why don't we come back later and finish." I wanted to hold him and feel close, but how romantic could we be in a dusty garage with the stench of oil and tires filling our noses? "I think we should stop this, said Tron." "What? Stop what?" "It's just beginning to be too much. I know we said this was just about sex, right? No feelings or nothing." I did say that. But of course that was before I fell in love with him. "Well we said we would tell each other when it was getting to be too much, and it's gotten to that point for me." I felt like someone dropkicked my heart, but I couldn't look bruised and hurt in front of him. "Okay cool." "So we're good?" Are we good? Hell no, we weren't good. I didn't even know what that question meant. "You can't make me cum at all...nothing. And you want this to be over?" Looking down at his phone, I saw Donesha's face. A picture of her on his home screen. When people did that, it meant only one thing. "So, you really love her?" "Come on man, with all of that. We said this wasn't permanent or nothing." I had fought with her my whole life, having to share everything

I had with her. And now I was taking something of hers without her knowing, yet he wanted to ruin this small victory in my life. "So that's it Tron? What about everything you told me?" But he wasn't even looking at me—his face was in his phone. She was calling, her name lighting up his screen, and without hesitation, he answered. "Hey baby….Yeah I'm just getting some extra water. Here I come." Just like that I was invisible. He was too busy straightening his clothes and talking to her to even notice me. "Alright. I'll be right in." He was off the phone but his expression didn't soften. "So we're good... like this is our last hurrah right." He grabbed an old rag, throwing it on the ground where he spilled his seed. "You know what...I'm good anyway. Don't know why I even gave you a chance." We're cool. Right?" It wasn't the regular breakup. It wasn't like I could say I'll see you around. In the next five minutes I was going to be seeing him in my mother's house. Just be cool. Be cool. He's testing you. He did that from time to time, told me that he was done fucking with me then on a late night I would get a text that he missed me and couldn't live without me. He hoisted the water on his shoulder and didn't even bother turning to look at me as he spoke. "Let me go out first," he said, not bothering to wait for me to answer. This, with cum stains drying on the garage floor, and my pussy wet and begging for more. This was the story of my life, getting left out in the cold, with no satisfaction from a man that I loved and happened to be sharing with my sister. I don't know how it started. We've been doing it so long it's hard to figure out at the exact point that I started fucking my Tron. It wasn't like I planned it, but now two years later here I am, sneaking back into the house after having my pussy filled in the garage. Except I felt even more empty than when I left the house. Tron said it was over, and now I felt numb; I didn't think him saying that was even possible. Back in the house it was business as usual—with aunts, uncles, cousins, and kids running about with no clue what I had just done. Music blaring, pots clanking, and enough talking that no one even noticed I was gone, except one person. "Where you been?" My sister was right there in my face, my twin. Looking at her was like staring in the mirror, except I looked way better. My hair was longer; she opted to chop hers off into a pixie cut that made her look like an alien. She was nothing like me—too vanilla—but somehow everyone loved her and I was the black sheep. "Just had to get something out of my car. Why?" She was all smiles, whispering like she was afraid someone would hear. "Come here...I need to talk to you." Sliding into the pantry off the kitchen, she started talking a mile a minute. "Slow down..." "Tron...I think...I think he's up to something." Hearing my man's name in her mouth raised my body temperature, but like everything in my life I shared it with my sister. "Really...like what?" I had to act surprised, nonchalant. "I don't know, he's been acting weird lately. Working a lot. I don't know, but I think he has a trip or something planned for me." A trip? The bitch didn't deserve a trip. I wanted to tell her the reason her man was missing was because he was in my bed every night he was at my place, but that would break her heart. Donesha wasn't hard like me. If she knew what was really going on, it would kill her—at least that's what Tron always told me. I can't tell her right now. When the time is right I'm going to leave her alone. Then we can be together. I've been dreaming of the fateful day for a year now. Watching and waiting for my turn to be happy, but now in this pantry I wanted to let the truth fly. I'm fucking your man, sis. He likes my pussy better than yours, get over it. I could taste the words like my mama's sweet potato pie, sweet in my mouth. I've wanted to tell her forever. Just one more month. He said he would tell her after Christmas. So instead of spilling the beans, I played along. "Oh, maybe he's just been working overtime." "You know, that's what I said. We're late on those bills too. Maybe that's it." She smiled. But I already knew why he was late on the bills. It wasn't easy taking care of my house and theirs too. "Alright y'all. Let's get ready to eat. Come on girls, grab a dish and bring it to the table." My mama peeked into the pantry, breaking up our time. "Mama, you rocking that red dress under that apron." She laughed, but it was the truth. My mother was the epitome of "black don't crack." "Thank ya, boo. Now come on. Let's get this dinner started." My Mom always did the holidays at our house, since it was the biggest.

She would cook the whole meal and not break a sweat. Tonight she was even glowing, sashaying into the dining room were a few dozen people crowded around. "Alright, now let's bless this food. Clarence, you do the honors this year." My stepfather stepped up with his salt-and-pepper beard and chiseled fireman's arms. "Alright, everyone find your seat and bow your heads." I found a seat and of course Donesha had to sit across from me. Tron sitting right next to her, I tried to make eye contact with him, but he didn't even glance my way. It was as if I didn't exist when she was around. Maybe it's an act. Keeping up appearances, I told myself. "Alright, everyone bow your heads… Dear Lord…" I bowed my head but I wasn't praying. Instead, I slipped off my shoe, reaching my foot across the table and right into Tron's lap. "Dear Lord, we thank you for our family. Bring us together safely Lord." I was thankful for the big dick that my foot was rubbing across, the man that it belonged to, and that one day the man would be mine. But looking into Tron's face, he wasn't enjoying it. His deep frown and the pushing of my foot made too much commotion. A few eyes opened, and mine slammed shut as I pulled my leg back across from under the table. "Now let us all say...Amen." The room erupted into Amens as dishes were immediately passed down the table. The long table that seated twenty people, the kids' table behind us, and a few stragglers eating in the living room and kitchen made the house sound like a stadium. But I felt all alone. There was no one here by my side. I was sitting across the table from the man I loved, but no one could know that except us. Just tell them. Tell everybody you love me, I silently begged Tron, wishing that he could hear my thoughts—but he didn't bother to look my way. Instead, he stood up and cleared his throat loudly. "Excuse me everyone. Can I have your attention please." It was like the earth stopped spinning when he spoke. I prayed he was going to do it, tell everyone he loved me right here at Thanksgiving. I sat up straight, smiling from ear to ear, but instead of Tron turning to me, he looked down to my sister. "Donesha, I love you with all of my heart. There is nothing that I wouldn't do for you and you are the best woman a man could have." When he smiled, his teeth were white as snow sparkling at everyone in the room. "Now tonight in front of everybody I want to tell them how much you mean to me." Rustling in his pocket, he reached for something, but he dropped to his knees so quick I could barely see what it was. "I love you, Donesha Hill. Will you marry me?" I couldn't have heard him right. I had to be dreaming, but while I was hyperventilating, my sister was screaming "yes" as the man I loved pushed a diamond ring onto her finger. The room was cheering, clapping, and screaming. Cameras flashed and everyone was happy. But not me. I watched them in shock as he hugged and kissed her. The tears streaming down her face were only matched by the tears coming down my own cheeks. The man that I wanted was marrying someone else—wait—not just someone else. He was marrying my sister and he did it right in front of my face. I wasn't sure, but this felt like war to me. Maybe he wants to see if you will fight for his love, I told myself, still in disbelief. "Can you believe it, your sister is going to get married," one of my aunts sitting next to me said, her face full of smiles and happy tears. I wanted to tell her "over my dead body" she would be getting married, but I didn't say a word. Instead, I smiled, a pretend fake smile stretched across my face as I planned my first attack—and that was telling her the truth.

Chapter Three
DONESHA

Tonight was a dream, something out of a movie. Driving home I couldn't stop staring at my new ring. Finally I was getting what I deserved. "Baby, you look at that thing anymore you are going to go blind," he told me, but I couldn't look away. "Look, this marks something new for us. No more games and lies. I'm going to be one hundred with you from now on." I tried to block the old Tron from my mind. The one that had me up crying all night mad and worried about the hoes that he was with. Now I had a ring on my finger, a new house, and a promise that he would be true. All I could do was accept him at his word. I smiled at him, tracing hearts in his hand, imaging the day we would be walking down the aisle. Months ago, I didn't even know if we would be able to be around each other, let alone getting married. "I really had no idea. This was a complete surprise." "You weren't supposed to. That's the way I planned it." This was a totally new Tron. Months ago he didn't plan shit but how to cheat on me. Now he was planning secret engagements. "Who knew...my mama... Lonnie...Who?" His face did this screwy frown when I said her name. "Your mom knew but Lanesha didn't know a thing." That wasn't a surprise. He hated my sister, couldn't stand her for some reason, and I knew the feeling was mutual on Lonnie's end. She didn't even say his name, she mostly called Tron "him" or some other pronoun, but never by name. "Come on...why do you hate my sister so much?" From the first time they met, Lanesha and Tron had been sworn enemies. She told me to leave his ass every chance she got, and tonight when he whipped out that ring she could barely tell me congratulations. "She's a hater. Did you see how she was looking at the table?" Rewinding back on the proposal, my emotions and thoughts were so high, I hadn't paid much attention to what my sister was doing. "She hugged me and said she was happy for me before we left." He sucked his teeth at that, pulling into the driveway. "I think she harbors some resentment toward you." This wasn't the first time he's said this and I still never understand what he's getting at. "What do you mean?" "You have a man, she doesn't. You and your mom fight, but that's because you are her favorite." I burst out in a deep laugh when he said that. "And...what does any of that mean?" "I'm just saying watch your sister. If she ever comes to you with some crazy shit, remember that we had this talk." He was always talking like this, telling me to watch Lonnie. "What about your mom. Does she know?" "Naw, I'll tell her one of these days." He said it like it wasn't a big deal. Like he went and bought new pants—not asked someone to be in his life. "One of these days?" "Baby, you know how Mom is...she's just..." "A bitch...a bitch is what she is." "That's my mom you're talking about." "Yeah, well she's a bitch. She never liked me and you probably didn't tell her you were proposing because she wouldn't approve." He took a deep breath, squeezing the wheel as he drove. I knew I touched a nerve but I didn't give a fuck. If he could talk about my sister, then I was going to tell him the truth about his bitter-ass mama. "I hope y'all can come together. We are going to be family." "That's the exact same way I feel about this issue you have with my sister." "That's different. Your sister is fucking evil." Lanesha was a spoiled-ass brat, but evil she wasn't. His mother's face was right beside "evil" in the dictionary, but I guess it's hard for him to notice it in someone that he shares blood with. "I think your reaching, Tron. I don't think my sister feels that way at all." He shook his head, pulling into our driveway. A brand-new, five-bedroom palace fit for a queen that I still wasn't used to yet, and now he popped me with another surprise. I guess when you get cheated on, this is the prize for staying. "Yeah whatever...you asked why I don't like her and that's my answer." Something about my sister always rubbed him the wrong way. I promised myself I was going to stay on some positive shit this year but I could tell he was pissed off.

"And what about Clarence, ole dry ass? He barely wanted to shake my hand." That sent off alarms in my head. I had to change the subject. "Well baby, it is what it is. Let's not worry about everybody else. Your Mom, Clarence, my sister...let's just go inside and celebrate us." I waited for him to lower the garage door and turn off the car, but instead he sat there staring at his phone. "Come on...let's go inside." I was ready to thank him for this big-ass diamond ring, but I had a feeling I wasn't going to get the chance. "Naw, I gotta go to work, remember? Black Friday—I gotta be there early." "I wanted to lie in bed for a little while...show you how happy I am about my ring." I felt like a toddler begging for my man to come lie down with me. "I know, boo, but that ring doesn't pay for itself." That was it, I get a ring but I have to pay for it with the absence of the man who gave it to me. It was always like this—the house gets built, we move in, then he's gone for two weeks straight—to a training course. "I'm store manager now, and we're in busy season. Gotta be ready." "But at a car dealership? What do you have to do to get ready?" "You know we open at five, and I gotta make sure the guys move the new cars into the showroom." It was creeping close to two o'clock a.m., and as much as I wanted him to stay, I knew the drill. It was always like this; I was in a relationship and soon to be wife of a workaholic who would neglect me at any moment to go make a dollar. "Gotta pay for this house, your tuition...I got a lot of shit on my plate and I don't need you complaining about how much I work." I hated being dependent on someone, and him throwing my tuition payment into the equation was enough to make me vomit. "Okay, okay, I get it. You don't have to pile things on—I told you I would pay you back. This is supposed to be a happy night." Tron just laughed. "When you become a doctor, then we can talk about you paying me back. For now, somebody has to pay these bills." Just that quickly, my good night was turning into a nightmare. "Whatever, Tron...I'm not complaining. I'm just..." "Just what?" "Nothing...don't worry about it." I felt like taking the ring off and giving it back. I was happier when we were broke, before he got this job at the dealership. We were much happier back then. "Alright then." He didn't even bother to look up from his phone. I got out of the car slowly, waiting for him to say he loved me, but instead he backed out of the driveway before I was even in the house. I had a ring and no man, just this big house. Walking into the kitchen, I turned on lights, unwrapping my take-home plate from my mom's when I heard a knock on the door. "You forget something boo...?" I yelled as I walked to the door. I hoped for once that maybe he was just joking and staying home after all. Pulling open the door instead of Tron's locs and a sweater, I was greeted by a greying beard and a leather coat. "Clarence...what are you doing here? Where is Mom?" "She's at those sales. That shit y'all do every year...that wait-in-line stuff." I looked around in a panic. It wasn't a good idea for him to be here. "We need to talk..." "Clarence I don't think..." "Come on, I know he's gone. I saw him drive off." I didn't have an excuse; there was no lie I could tell. "Come on and let your pops inside. It's cold out here." I hated when he called himself that. He was far from my father. "Yeah, come in Clarence." I corrected him. There was no need to call him pops or dad. He was my mother's husband and that was as far as the relation went. "So, congrats on the engagement." He half-laughed as he said it, his voice dripping in sarcasm like he was telling a joke. He peeled off his leather coat, and the tight shirt underneath showed every muscle on his body. "You shouldn't be here." I told him. "Why not? Why can't I come see and check on you." "Because...you know what that leads to." He didn't say a word. Instead, he went to the kitchen. "I'm going to get a glass of water. You want something?" I wanted him to go, but I simply shook my head no, following behind him a few feet away. "Dinner was good tonight. It was good seeing everyone." he walked around my kitchen like this was his house. Opening cabinets, getting water from the pitcher in the fridge, then leaning against the counter. "Yeah it was nice seeing everyone." I didn't mention my surprise; I knew that would only turn this conversation in a direction I didn't want it to go. "Yeah...and that ring. That's a big ring." He said, putting down his glass. "Can I see it?" He didn't wait for me to answer. Instead, he stepped closer, taking my hand. Just him touching me sent my heart fluttering and spinning a million miles a minute. "Damn...it's pretty." he said "I could have given you one bigger." "Clarence...I..." before I could say another word, his lips were on mine. "Clarence..." "How you gonna marry him huh? You're supposed to be waiting for me." That was our plan. He would divorce Mama and we would run away together. But that was a plan five years overdue. I wasn't getting any younger, and sneaking around wasn't at the top of my list anymore. Pushing back out of his embrace, I stood my ground. "I can't wait for you forever. We had our time and it was wrong. I realize that now. I'm going to marry Tron and we will put all of this to bed." But instead, he pulled my left hand down to his zipper. His rock-hard dick was damn near exploding out of his pants. "Tell my dick that. Tell him that you are going to marry that punk and leave this dick...you know he's yours right? My dick belongs to you." I wanted to tell Clarence and his dick to leave but my body wouldn't let a sound come out. I missed him. I missed the way he touched and held me. It started out as revenge on my mama, but somehow my and Clarence's relationship translated into so much more. "Yeah...I already know you can't." The smile across his face was like he had me. He knew me too well. "I know he can't please you like I can." He was right about that, but I didn't want to tell him. It would have put lighter fluid on the already blazing ego that was Clarence Turner. "Clarence, we said we wouldn't do this anymore." I was begging like a child not to do this—not demanding—because I was powerless to him. And like every other time, he didn't listen and I was powerless to stop him. His lips on my neck came first, and then he was picking me up. My legs straddled around his waist as he held me up with ease and kissed me like I was the last woman on earth. "I love you...don't you know that? I love you..." He repeated it so much, I started to believe him. Over and over again he said the words as he sat me down on the marble counter top. Dropping to his knees I knew what was coming next—the spreading of my legs and my bare pussy right at his eye level. I felt his warm tongue parting my pussy lips, sending me straight to heaven with a diamond ring on my finger and a certified pussy monster between my legs. My eyes were rolling and calling out for God as Clarence did tongue maneuvers with my clit. I saw Heaven, zooming through clouds with mountains of orgasm hitting my pussy lips—when I heard the familiar mechanical voice. "FRONT DOOR," the alarm sounded, telling me that the front door had opened and so had the gates to hell.

Chapter Four

LANESHA

I was going to tell her the truth. My sister needed to know that I was fucking this man that was going to be her fiancé My blood began to boil thinking of Tron fucking her right in front of me, but when my eyes focused, I saw the salt-and-pepper beard dripping with my sister's pussy juices didn't belong to my man at all. "Clarence….Donesha…?" I felt like I was about to throw up. Donesha always played the goody two-shoes and now I had caught her doing some shit that not even God would forgive. Donesha had her legs wide open, head back and eyes rolling and between her thighs was good ole Clarence. He looked like some pervert from a porno.

"What are you doing here...how did you get in?" Donesha asked, scrambling to cover herself. "Where is Mama?" I thought about telling her she was right behind me. "The key you gave me, remember?...we're going shopping—you told me to come over..." Clarence couldn't even look at me. He scrambled to his feet, wiping his face as Donesha jumped down from the counter. "Where is your mother?" "She's at the fucking store waiting on us." I told him. "Please don't tell your mother." He had the audacity to ask me that with my sisters pussy still fresh on his breath. "That's all you have to say to me is 'don't tell Mom'?" I couldn't believe what I was seeing, but after the shit I've done, on second thought I could. All the times I've fucked Tron at a family gathering just because it felt fun to be that dangerous. I played with fire and for some reason I always thought my sister was too much of a goody two-shoes...not anymore. "With Clarence... really, Donesha." I wished I had a gun on me. I would have shot him right through his frosted beard for playing my mama, but a part of me could see why. Clarence was fine as fuck. "I'm sorry...I..." His weak ass started stuttering like some retarded fool. "Please...it was a mistake." "A mistake. So you just fell head-first into my sister's pussy?" Both of them looked to the floor. This was the bitch he wanted to marry. Tron skipped over me and was going to marry this bitch. "I always knew you liked her more than me." I laughed at all the Christmases he gave her an extra special gift, and now I knew why. "How long has this been going on?" "Sis...I can explain." Donesha finally said something, but I wasn't trying to hear it. Phone-in-hand, I pulled it up and they both jumped like they had seen a ghost. "I said...HOW LONG HAS THIS BEEN GOING ON? Tell me that, or tell it to Mom." Clarence bucked up, taking a step toward me, and I took two steps backwards. "Look. Your mom doesn't have to know." he kept walking forward, his belt buckle jingling with his every step as I backed up toward the door. "Clarence...what the hell are you doing?" Donesha screamed after him, but his eyes were trained on me. "Get the fuck away from my sister." I could hear her opening a drawer and getting a knife but I had something way better than that. "She's going to tell, and

Yvette doesn't need to know about this." Reaching into my purse, I pulled out my Beretta, flicking it off safety. "Don't take another step toward me motherfucker, or I'm going to blow your brains out." I meant every word, until I saw him move. It was instinct, my finger sliding to the trigger and pulling. It happened so quick that I couldn't move until I heard screams.

Chapter Five

TRON

I thought a gun was firing as I pulled up to the dealership. But the noise was coming from a brand new Chevy Drop Top at the entrance. It was the middle of the night, but the whole crew was in with the lights on, moving cars like this was a regular day. The whole team at Onyx Chevrolet were real straight go-getters, but it wasn't a surprise. The weakest person on the team still made six figures. The guys in the parts and repair shop made at least sixty grand a year. There was money seeping out everywhere and it coaxed a team of men to head out to work on a cold morning. Walking up, it made me feel proud to be the manager of the dealership.

"Boy, it sounds sweet." It may have been the dark of night, but the dealership was lit up like a Christmas tree. We were pulling out all the stops this year, and this bright red Chevy sitting by the door was really going to turn some heads. "Yeah, we're going to set it up by the entrance and move the other cars around it." Ro said as I got to the entrance. They were already here and working. I was the lone straggler boss just getting in for our busiest day of the year. "Man, what the fuck is that on your pants." I wasn't expecting that to be the first thing I heard when I headed into work. I really didn't think anybody would notice. Side-stepping my partner, I tried to look away as I told him the lie "I spilled some damn food on it. I'm about to change." But he was already laughing as he followed me into my office. "You still fucking her, aren't you?" It wasn't a secret to Ro; he was the only one I could tell about shit like this, but I still played it off. "Who?" I went into my connecting bathroom to get away from his ass but Ro followed me anyway right to the door. I had to damn near close it in his face. Standing right outside the door so I could hear him, he told my whole damn life.

"Your girlfriend's sister, that's who, nigga. Don't try to play, you told me that shit was over." He didn't understand. Ro was ten years older than me; he still had some of that old-school mentality in him. "You got too many distractions from what we trying to do. T. Can't have this shit or you're gonna jeopardize the program." Program this and that. It was all he ever talked about. "Man you need to get some pussy. I'm not putting our shit in jeopardy, I'm just having some fun." "Yeah, whatever man." He didn't believe me, but that's because he's been fucking the same pussy for fifteen years. Going home to the same woman faithfully. Me, on the other end, I needed variety. "Bruh, you just don't know how fat her ass was looking today." I thought back to entering the house. Yeah Donesha looked bad, but when I saw her sister, it looked like she had two melons in the back of her dress. I told myself that I was going to break it off today and leave it alone but I had to have one more test drive. "But you bought the ring. You said you were going to ask old girl to marry you tonight..." That was the funny part. Opening the door, I walked out like Mack of the year, in my tailored suit a pair of all-black Louboutins on my feet like I was going to the player's ball. "I did propose. Ain't shit change in my plan." His jaw damn near hit the floor as I said it. "Nigga...how the fuck you propose to your girl with your side piece right there." Ro was laughing but this was the shit that I did all the time. "Because, nigga. I'm a motherfucking pimp. I do what the fuck I want." Ro hadn't known me that long but I did this shit for fun. I could fuck with a bitch's head in my sleep and just because I found the one in Donesha didn't mean I didn't want an appetizer in her sister. "Man you gotta break that shit down to me because I can't even begin to understand." Ro plopped down on the couch in my office like he was an eager student about to take notes. "It's easy, bruh. She got this competition shit going on with her sister and she been wanting to give me the pussy." "How the fuck you know that?" I thought back on when I found out that Donesha was a twin, I was looking to see somebody that was sort of favoring her but the shit was so heavy at first that I couldn't tell them apart. Sometimes things happen, and honestly, that's how the shit happened. "It kind of fell in my lap, bruh. You know we was up drinking for Mardi Gras, Donesha got drunk as shit and was tired, so she went to bed leaving me and her sister and…" "You wild nigga…you wild as fuck." I just shrugged, thinking back on that night. We were talking and vibing, and the next thing I know I leaned over and kissed her. A kiss turned into a French kiss, a rub turned into taking her shirt off, and things just progressed until I was fucking her while my girl was asleep in the next room. "Shit, I told her it wouldn't last forever. There had to be a cap on this shit or she was going to be fucking me forever." "Man, but you straight dirty with it. You know chicks can be vindictive." I was already on top of that; I had an exit plan already worked out. "I never text her, it's only phone calls. And I'm already getting it into Donnie's head that the bitch is jealous. So if she ever tries to come out her mouth sideways about me she'll know to block that shit." "You wild boy. Better be careful, that shit is going to bite you in the ass one day." It was a warning from a nigga that didn't have a Mack game like me. He knew nothing about women or how to play this game. "You know they been talking about you." "Who…?" "Them white boys that have been here for a while. You know them motherfuckers wanna see you shine. And you got this side-business shit that they aren't happy about." "Man, fuck them." "I'm just saying you been doing too…" Before he could finish, my phone started buzzing. "Damn, my alarm won't set. Shit supposed to work from my phone." "Better get to that alarm, guy. Gotta protect your business." they laughed at me when I bought into the franchise but I knew this shit wasn't going to last forever. "Whatever…It's just telling me the door was open." Looking through the cameras, what I saw made my eyes damn near pop out of my head. "What the hell is wrong?" "It's Donesha's sister. She's standing on the front porch." Shit looked like something off a movie. The cameras I had, only pointed outside the house. "Why the hell is she there?" I dialed Donesha don't trying to question shit else. I needed to know what was happening or everything I worked for was about to fall.

Chapter Six

LANESHA

I reached into my purse pulling out my Beretta. "Don't take another step toward me Clarence, and I mean it. I flicked the gun off safety and held it down, but I was ready for business. "Put that away; we're family."

"No, 'we' aren't family. Me, my sister, and my mom— we're family. You're an outsider...you should be fucking ashamed...both of you." I wanted to laugh in their faces but I kept a steel face of anger. Inside, though, my heart was jumping like a damn trampoline. I backed towards the door, leaving them alone. They were both shaking like leaves, and with this gun in my hand, I needed to go. "Now I'm leaving....go back to whatever you're doing."

My original plan was to come over here and tell Donesha the truth. That her man loved me, that I was the one he wanted to be with and this proposal was just his guilty conscience. She deserved to know the truth, but now I had a whole different scenario playing in my head. "But sister…wait…please…please don't tell Mom." Donesha was the most hilarious when she got like this. "It will kill her. Please don't tell." I didn't say a word. Instead I backed out of the house, slamming the door behind me and running to my car. I burned rubber away from the house through the streets under blackened skies. I breezed through stop signs and blinking lights until I hit the freeway with my phone ringing. "Hello…" I answered without looking at the phone. "What the hell is going on?" Tron asked his voice blasting through the Bluetooth system of my car. "Nothing…why." "I saw you on the cameras at the house." I wanted to laugh at that. His wife fiancé was fucking Clarence but here he goes calling me. "I was there with my sister. What business is it of yours?" "Look…I told you this would never been serious and…" I stopped listening to him instead I was in my own mind figuring out what I just saw and that's when it hit me. I was right. I was right this whole damn time and finally I caught her ass. I knew there was no way she wasn't fucking someone else. Tron thought she was so devoted and true to him, but I knew my sister. At her core she is a vindictive bitch. Now I knew I was right, my laughs filling the car as my plan came together. "Hello…do you hear me Lanesha?" I knew with all the time that Tron was working, or with me, that my sister was getting her itch scratched by someone else. Who knew it would be the man I called my stepfather? "Tron I'm busy. Talk to you some other time." I hung up on his ass. Letting him sit in doubt and fear was the best revenge I could give his ass. The fact that he called me and not my sister was proof enough that his dumb ass had no clue about the truth. "Yeah Clarence, I knew your ass was up to something slick, but with my sister." I could only shake my head. "My sister, now I have proof," I said to the car as I played back the video from my cellphone. Neither of the dummies paid attention to my hands as I ruined their little lovemaking session. Now my Sister, Clarence, and Tron were all blowing my phone up, calling back to back as I tried to watch the video and drive. This was beyond funny to me. But I answered for one of them. "Hello…" "Lonnie…please come back so I can talk to you. Please don't tell Mom…" She was crying hysterically but telling Mom was the last thing I had plans for. "I think you need to reevaluate your life, Nene. Especially since you just got engaged. This isn't fair to Tron." I wanted to burst into laughter but I was able to keep it believable. "I know…I know…I just…" "Look I'm going shopping. I'll talk to you later." "What mall are you at. I'll come meet you." Now she wanted to be around me. "No… just stay at home. I need some space." That shocked her, and the line went mute. "Space…from me?" Donesha couldn't believe it, since in our twenty-five years I've never asked her for space. "Yes…from you. I need to think. Don't call me, I'll call you…" With that, I hung up and started back into my fit of laughter. My sister wasn't going to see what I had in store for her ass, but it was going to be a magnificent show. "I always get what I want, little sister. This has nothing to do with you…it's all about me." I hate to be humiliated and that's what Tron did. He proposed to my sister right in my face while I still had the stench of his dick permeating my pussy. "You can't quit me nigga, until I'm ready to be quit. You're going to marry me...bet that," I screamed throughout the car like he was inside with me. I had a plan—-a long-stretch plan. It came to me as soon as I saw Tron get on his knees and propose to that bitch. I loved my sister, but she was a spoiled, fucking brat since we were kids. She cried and somehow the sky opened and she got everything she wanted. We were twins, but I'm the oldest by a few minutes and sometimes that felt like a few years. She was always talking about how evil Granny was, how life was so fucked up for us, and here she is doing the same evil shit. Our mom would be devastated if she found out that her precious Clarence, her gift from God, was sneaking around—especially with her own daughter. Driving to the mall, I felt like I was the chess master holding all the pieces. I just had to play my part right. I found a parking spot and tried to breathe, calm my nerves and make sure my gun was back on safety. The last thing I needed was to shoot my damn self when I now had so much to live for. Knocks on my window revealed the woman in the middle of all this, my mother. I unlocked the doors and she jumped in, full of smiles and energy. If only she knew what the hell I knew. "Whew...it's cold out there." She looked around and soon her smile faded. "Where is your sister?" She didn't want to know that. "She's excited about that ring. You know how she is. I couldn't get her out the house." "Oh, that was beautiful. I knew a little something but I didn't think he would do it at Thanksgiving,." Lanesha laughed as her phone rang. Her mother didn't deserve this. She was a good woman who worked hard. Now that she finds love, Donesha does what she does best, steal her joy. "Oh, it's Nene." Yvette answered the phone with "Hey baby girl. How you feeling, you newly engaged woman?" Donesha was checking temperatures. She wanted to know if her sister had told Mommy apparently, but she wouldn't tell, at least not now. "Oh yeah, we're here now at the store. Lonnie said you were at home with your man." Mama laughed. She was so hip like that, but she wasn't hip enough to be sharing her husband. A text message came through, breaking up my ear hustling. "How much to make this go away?" It was from Clarence, whose pockets were deeper than his devotion to my mother. I hadn't even begun to think about a number. "Alright, baby. You get some rest and we'll see you in a few hours at the other sale. We're about to hit these early bird stores." This was my mother's tradition. Her happiest time was spending money. "I'll let you know…" was my only response to her husband. Right now I needed to calculate how much this information cost. "Alright now daughter, it's just me and you. Let's go get in those lines." She laughed without a clue. She didn't know what I just saw. "Alright, let's go ma…" Getting out of the car, she talked my head off all the way to the line, but my mind was on my phone. "10k…" was the reply from Clarence. I didn't say a word. My silence could be bought but it would take a whole lot more than ten thousand dollars. More like ten thousand years with Tron, because if I couldn't have him, money ceased to matter.

Chapter Seven
YVETTE

"Teen pregnancy is NOT a death sentence." The poster was of a very pregnant teenage girl peeling out of a prison uniform. I couldn't take my eyes off of it, maybe because I was an inmate of teen pregnancy once. But I got a double dose, twin girls at the age of fifteen when most girls my age were just getting purity rings. I was running wild at fifteen. The streets were my home. With my mama away at rehab and my Daddy locked up, I had to keep the bills paid and take my ass to school. I was too young to even get a job, and if I didn't go to school I already knew that DFS would come get me and I would be in foster care. I couldn't have that so there was only one thing for me to do, From one dope boy to the next, I bounced around from bed to bed to pay my bills and stay laced. They all had promises of love but none of it ended up that way. Ditching that program, I got into a shelter, and all seemed to get better until my clothes stopped fitting and I couldn't stop feeling hungry. Fifteen and scared, I knew something wasn't right, so I went to a free clinic and my life changed forever. An hour after walking through the door, I got my best birthday gift ever, I found out I was pregnant—and not just with one baby—but four months along with twins. That day, I walked out of the office knowing two things. That I was going to be a mom, and from now on I would never be alone. People talk about the homeless with their smelly clothes or incessant begging, but the biggest problem I had was the loneliness. There was no mother for me to go crawl to, no dad to protect me from the big bad guys on the street. Instead it was just me, and at that point it changed from just me to me and my babies. Exactly twenty-five years later, I'm forty years old and it feels like the time flew by.

My girls went from little babies to grown women and I changed from a girl to a woman my damn self. All the hard times, nights filled with more wants than I could afford, and then my mama got clean and our lives changed. She came back, begging to be in our lives. "Is there anything I can do to help you? Anything!" she begged and pleaded at my door. I had just been fired from my job, was a month behind on my rent, and the only job offer I had was in another state. I couldn't take the girls, but if I stayed I would be broke. "I have one thing to ask you. Can you stay here, stay clean, and take care of my girls. I will send you back money. I just need someone to watch them while I work, okay?" It was simple. I waited and watched what she would say. With tears flowing down her face and the girls fighting to sit on her lap, she gave me her answer. "Yes, I will protect them with everything in me." I breathed a sigh of relief. I loved my mother, and I wanted to believe that she would watch after my girls while I made some money. I was able to leave the girls with her, go out of state, and get a good job to send money back home. All of that hard work paid off, and today is my birthday. But instead of spending it out at lunch with my girls or on a cruise with my husband, I'm in the doctor's office getting my 'forty and fabulous' checkup. "Oh my goodness...it's your birthday." This doctor was new, and smiling from ear to ear. I grimaced at her fake smile. My doctor—my real doctor—would have given me a hug and made genuine conversation. With this lady, I felt like nothing more than a number. "So how does it feel to be forty?" The doctor was making small talk as she took notes while I sat in the room naked, wrapped in a paper-thin gown I couldn't believe it myself. "You don't look forty. If I wasn't looking at your chart I would have thought you were in your twenties." I almost took her question as a slight, but now that she delivered this compliment I felt a little bit better. Forty years old with two grown daughters, a husband, a new career, and skin that kept me looking young—what more could a person want? "Honestly, I feel great. I feel better than I did after my divorce." I laughed to keep from crying, because what I said was the lie that I told everyone. To the outside world I was okay and everything was great, but something was nagging at me. Inside I felt like I was dying, my chest felt empty like someone had stolen my heart. I was loved but I couldn't help but have this feeling that I was missing something. But I was in the wrong doctor's office to talk about this. I needed a psychiatrist, not a gynecologist. "Well that's good to hear. How about your health. Are you concerned with anything?" I wish I didn't have to tell her this. My body was doing some weird things as I approached forty. "Well, there is one. I have this odor...just out of nowhere." her eyes got big when I said that. Scribbling on her notepad I could see the wheels of diagnosis turning in her head. She was a young doctor, with blonde hair and wire-rimmed glasses. She wasn't my first choice for a doctor but my own had retired, so here I was with this fresh-from-medical-school-wet-behind-the-ears physician. Just get through this and you won't have to see her for another year. "Yeah, I figure it's probably my pH balance changing or something. I'm sure it's nothing to worry about." I laughed it off, but the doctor wasn't taking this as a joke. "How about your partner—has he complained of anything?" Now I was confused. How did me coming here to talk about my pussy getting older have anything to do with my husband? I wanted to snap on her. The little bitch probably thought I was some whore out there running the streets. She tapped the side of her clip board with her pen impatiently awaiting my response, but I had to take an extra second. If I said what was on my mind then I would have to find a new doctor. All black women aren't sluts, bitch...but instead I was a bit more cordial. "What does my husband have to do with this?" "Well it may be sexual transmitted or…" "No, no, no...let me stop you there." I took a deep breath, looking this young doctor square in her beady-ass eyes. "it's probably just a yeast infection or my pH is off, like I said." Staring her down, I looked straight through her. It was always young bitches like this that swore they knew everything, but couldn't tell their pussy from a hole in the wall. "Right...just trying to narrow down the possible issues..." she stammered, breaking eye contact and going back to her notes. She was a young doctor, probably fresh out of medical school. "Now, I know I'm a new patient with you since Doctor Goldstein retired. But I don't have STD problems. I am married….m-a-r-r-i-e-d…so yeah, it's not that." "Okay. I'm sorry if I offended you. I tell you what—let me go get the nurse. When I get back, we can take a sample and confirm you're what you said. She left, and the "what ifs" started to creep into my brain. What if it was an STD? I had to laugh at the thought. There was no way it was that. Me and Clarence fucked like rabbits; how would he have time to be with anyone else? "Knock knock…" The doctor was back. I couldn't even bother to smile at her, but luckily she had a nurse with her. "All right, go ahead and sit back while I put your legs in the stirrups." It was the same thing every year, and no matter how many pap smears I'd had, it never got easier. No woman wants to spread her legs and not get any reward from it. "All right. We're going to take a few cultures from the pap smear and just an extra one, so I can look under the microscope here at the office, okay?" "Fine." Folding my arms and clasping my hands, I let her do a small dig-around in my pussy. "All right, we're done. You can go ahead and get dressed and we'll be right back." As I sat up, they both ran out of the room like they had seen a ghost. Hell, the smell wasn't that bad. Just a little different than normal. What if Clarence is cheating? I thought about it as I got dressed. Slipping on my clothes, I thought about how he begged me to marry him. How he'd come to my house every day to sit with me on the porch to tell me how much he wanted to take me on a date. That happened for months before I allowed it. A man like that wouldn't cheat on you. That sealed the deal for me. Now fully dressed, I waited for what felt like forever until the knocks came again. "All right, sorry to keep you, Ms. Stanton. I had one of the other doctors take a look as well just to be sure." "Take a look at what?" Cancer, it must be cancer. My mother died of it and so did my grandma, and ever since, my mind was wrapped around the 'C word' tighter than a python to its prey. "Well, it looks like you have Trichomoniasis." "Trich-a-what?" "It's a sexually transmitted disease." As she said it, my mouth went dry. Every part of my body went numb. She was talking, but my mind was miles and miles away. I felt like my body was flipped upside down and shaken like a snow globe. When she slid a prescription in my hand, I felt like it weighed fifty pounds. "Get this filled and have your husband get checked out as well." She smiled but I knew the grin was an "I told you so." "We'll send out the results of your pap but I'm sure it will come back positive because of the disease. So, take the medicine and come back in a month so we can redo your pap." She was still smiling while I was dying inside. I could say nothing. Instead I walked out with my head low and a prescription in my hand. In the car I finally gained the feeling back in my fingers and was able to make a call. "Hey baby...you ready to come home and get some of this birthday loving." On a normal day, I would have been excited for my husband to answer the phone that way. But right now I felt sick and ready to throw up. "Who have you been fucking, Clarence." The words spewed out like hot lava. "What? What are you talking about?" "I just left the doctor. I have a fucking STD!" I screamed louder than I thought was possible. So loud, that people walking through the parking lot stared at me like I was the antichrist. "Wait, wait baby...what are you talking about, an STD? There must be a mistake." "What fucking mistake could it be, Clarence?" "Baby. You gotta believe me. I'm not sleeping with anyone. I promise…I love you." "You're sure…you're one hundred percent sure?" I asked him, my eyes darting from the penicillin prescription and back to the phone. "Baby, on my life. I would never cheat on you." "Fine…I'm on my way home. We're going to get to the bottom of this." "Hell yeah. What's the name of it. Let me start looking it up." I told him what it was, even spelled it per some damn handout the bitch of a doctor gave me. "Alright, baby…come on home and we can talk this out." I didn't say a word. If this man was cheating on me, so help me God, I was going to jail for the rest of my life.

Chapter Eight

CLARENC

When you get married, all the mystery stops. There is no more coming home to a butt-naked woman with her ass hanging out of some Victoria's Secret panties. Instead, it is granny panties, bonnets covering up rollers, and for dinner it is a microwaved plate of mush. I tried to deal with it, be a good guy and roll with the punches while my wife shunned me and neglected my needs, but a man can only take so much. Somewhere along the line I got tired of that, got sick of begging my wife to fuck me in the house that I paid for. A man's got needs and desires that needed to be filled. Unfortunately, sometimes I went to go get those needs handled by bitches that weren't so clean. Now it was all blowing up in my face. "I can't believe this...I can't fucking believe this." My wife paced the floor behind me. "I almost got it, baby…" I was trying to save my marriage. my fingers working faster over the keyboard as she stomped harder across the floor behind me. With every second that passed by, I knew she was thinking and wondering. If she thought too hard, she would start to connect the dots. Was I really working late, why did I have a code on my phone, what were those mysterious stains on my shirts, was I really working during those week-long trips? It was too much to question, and if she found out all the shit I was doing, I could kiss my retirement, pension, and savings goodbye. It's cheaper to keep her, and in this case I had no option but to keep her or be broke for the rest of my life. So here I was, looking for solutions to our problem online. Something that could tell her that the STD she had didn't come from me. "See, baby. It says here you can catch it from dirty washcloths or hot tubs. We were in that hot tub a few weeks ago at the hotel. Isn't that when you said everything started?" I crossed my fingers hoping this was it. I was on the computer looking for anything, any possible reason besides the fact that I had been slipping my dick in another twat. A few other twats—rather, several other twats—shit, who the fuck was counting anyway? I was fucking whoever I wanted; if she wasn't going to give me the pussy then I had to get it from somewhere. "Yeah...it did start around then. Do you really think that's it?" "I don't know, babe. It could be." I kept wiping my face, praying to God that I wasn't sweating bullets while I was looking for an alibi. "You see, it also says here that it can lie dormant in your body for years. Maybe you have had it for years and didn't know?" "Really?" She came over to the screen, squinting her eyes trying to read it. Sure enough, there was the information that was about to save my life. I watched her face soften as she read the paragraph on the doctor site a few times. "Dammit. I can't believe this." I had her; it was over now. All I had to do was smooth this shit over. "I'm so embarrassed. I can't believe this." "Baby, it's okay. Come here." I wrapped my arms around her and pulled her down into the chair with me. "There is nothing to be embarrassed about." "But I accused you of cheating and it's probably me with the damn problem. Shit!" She was damn near in tears and I was breathing a sigh of relief. "I feel so stupid." "Baby...no need to feel stupid. It's an honest reaction. Hell, I would have reacted the same way." I wouldn't have. Instead, I would go to the doctor and get the problem fixed and not say a damn word, which was exactly what I did when I found out I had the shit a couple weeks ago. "I just feel horrible, and for this shit to happen on my birthday..." "MOM, YOU HERE?" Hearing her voice made my dick jump. Something about fucking her and parading around Yvette like nothing was going on excited me. "Yeah baby, we're up here." The mystery of infidelity was the spark that my life needed. Something about fucking these different women and my wife being oblivious excited me. "I'll stay down here." "Ugh...I don't understand why you two can't get along?" We played the game and played it well. Yvette thought I couldn't stand her daughter—and vice versa—but that was the furthest thing from the truth. "That's all on your daughter. But hey, look...are you going to tell them about the money?" "I don't know. Been thinking about waiting for a while—talk to some financial advisors so they don't blow it all in one day." It sounded like music to my ears, but I still had to be cool about shit. "Why?" "I was just asking—didn't know if you needed my support or something, because I was going to leave out." That sounded believable that I was being the supportive husband. "Aww baby, thank you but I'm good." "MA!" "I'm coming, dammit." She played the bratty daughter that hates her stepfather so well that I almost believed it at times. But acting like that only pushed me to make her take extra dick when we did get together. "She's going to be here for a while. We're going to wrap presents. Maybe I should cancel." "No." This was my time to get away. I needed to go handle some business, and her being here with her daughter was the perfect way out. "Naw baby, don't be down. This is really no big deal," I whispered in her ear, as I guided her down the stairs. "You just take those antibiotics and you'll be fine. No worries, right?" A smile and a nod from her, and I felt like it was all over. Then I saw her. Donesha, in the kitchen, bent over in the refrigerator. "Hello Donesha." "Hi…" She gave a dry reply but luckily we didn't have to fake an interaction today. My phone rang as I walked down behind Yvette.

"Girl, get yo butt out of my refrigerator." "Mom, I'm hungry." She pouted, and there Yvette was—flying around the kitchen to cook her something. "I'm gone, okay…" "Okay baby. I love you." "Love you more…" As I kissed her, my mind was in a few other places. I bypassed Donesha like she didn't exist, and headed for my car just in time to hear my phone ringing. The name on the screen said it all. BB for "bigger bitch," yet I answered it anyway. "Hello…" Voice barely above a whisper, I answered the call. Even in the garage by myself I had to make sure I wasn't heard. "So, you been dodging me." "Naw, I'm not dodging you, I've just…" In the car I could talk normal again while waiting on the garage door to open. "Been playing house, right. Sitting on the money that you owe me. Do we need to go back to court?" Court, the last place I wanted to see. "Why—so you can get more alimony out of me or something? What, you need a new ass and some more titties? Just let me know." She was always asking for more of something, my greedy ex-wife who couldn't take no for an answer. "Yeah, whatevah." "And I'm not playing house…this is my house. You know I'm married." She laughed, but I didn't find shit funny. "Come on now, Clarence. You know that dick is always going to belong to me." I shuddered when she said it. There was nobody that could suck dick like my first wife, taking my cum to the back of her throat and swallowing it like it gave her life. "Whatever, man...I don't want to hear that shit. I'm coming over there for one reason and one only." "Yeah, but does your wife know about me?" That was a good question. There was the truth and then there was a lie, so I opted for the lie as I backed out of the driveway. "What does that have to do with anything?" She laughed at me. The devilish villain-like laugh usually reserved for movie bad guys was now coming out of my phone. "Because I wonder does she know you fucked me the other night." She laughed. "That you were cheating on her with me, and right when I was going to expose your ass, you come up with an envelope full of money." She laughed some more as I left my house in the rearview. Nothing was funny about the cat she was trying to let out of the bag. "Look, I told you I was going to pay you what I owe you. All that other shit is between me and you. You need to keep your teeth closed on that." "What about that dick?" It was a hot commodity right now, but my dick was what got me into this situation in the first place. "You gave me a fucking disease...you think I'm going to still fuck with you after that." She laughed, but again I didn't find shit funny. Yvette could have kicked me out for that shit, ended the marriage, my accounts would have been closed—and then what? "Aww, you know this pussy is too good to give up. Plus I told you that was a mistake...just a little bacterial infection that got out of control." "Got out of control...bitch..." Before I could finish my sentence, a few beeps filled the line. It was Yvette. "Hold on a second..." Without waiting, I was on the line with my wife. "Yeah boo..." "I can't believe this shit!" she screamed. "Believe what...?" "This is the craziest bullshit I have ever seen in my life, Clarence. This is horrible. I can't fucking believe this! My heart dropped to the floor. She knew...I could tell...my wife knew everything.

Chapter Nine

DONESHA

"I know it who it is…I know exactly who the fuck it is! How could you do this…" You would have thought she found out I was fucking her man, but no. My mama was on the porch, stomping around like a toddler because somebody took her Christmas decorations. "This is a damn shame. People work hard for their things and bastards come and steal them." I watched as she stomped back and forth, not sure whether to hide or run as she screamed on the front porch like a maniac and I loved every second of it. "I'm tired of people taking my SHIT!" she screamed with the phone to her ear, her husband on the line making promise after promise to calm her down. "Ma, it's just some damn ornaments. Stop being so dramatic." "I'm not being dramatic. Someone stole my damn ornaments out of the front yard. This is the second time it's happened." My mother has always been very particular about things. A crumb could be out of place and she would notice, so ornaments missing from her perfect little Christmas display had her panties bunched tighter than Mike Tyson's fist. "Did you notice that they were gone, Clarence?" Clarence couldn't notice shit, but my ass he damn sure wasn't checking for no Santa ornaments and fake stuffed reindeer. From the look on her face I could tell Clarence didn't know shit, and the way her lip was turned up made me think of my granny. My granny had us cleaning her house all the time. If she thought a crumb was out of place we would wake up out of our beds and clean the whole house or else. She probably got all this crazy-ass obsession from our grandma, because that bitch would make us clean the house from top to bottom every damn day. She had dozens of little trinkets and glass figurines that she demanded we dust and clean by hand weekly. Like a prison warden, Granny would walk around in an old tattered robe, staring down on us with a horse whip in her hands. Anytime we made a mistake, the whip would crack and leave a welt so thick that she would have to keep us at home from school for a week so no one would see. "I'm going to get a damn alarm, Clarence. I'm tired of this shit. I want to know who the hell keeps coming up to my damn house and stealing shit!" She screamed into the phone. He probably thought her ass was batshit crazy, but this was the wife he chose. "Do what you have to do baby. I gotta go, I got work to do." He was on speaker, his voice invading our space. Sometimes I loved to hear him and other times hearing his voice made my skin crawl. Right now was one of those times when I didn't have to fake being annoyed. "Hang up, what is he supposed to do?" I tried snatching the phone from her to hang it up, but she pulled it away. "Young lady...what the hell is wrong with you?" I didn't have an answer; it would have taken too long for me to tell her. "I'm just trying to wrap these damn gifts with you and you're flying off about some ornaments. What is wrong with you?" Her face softened as I said it. "Clarence...I'll call you later." She hung up, shaking her head. "Come on, let's go back in the house." I followed her inside, her head hanging so low I thought it was going to wipe the floor. "You know, I've never really had that many girlfriends, so I'm not the best with talking about my feelings." I felt the apology coming on, the one I'd been waiting for my whole life. Finally she is going to recognize how much of a dumpster-trash parent she was. "But you girls are grown now, so I feel like we should be best friends. So I can share this with you." I sat down on the floor, surrounded by gifts and wrapping paper waiting for her to speak. "I have a disease..." "A what?" This wasn't what I was expecting. "Trichomonas or some shit. I went to the doctor today and she told me." She started to tear up a bit as she explained. "Naturally, I thought it was Clarence, but he promised he hasn't done anything. Plus we found out that it can lay dormant in the body, so who knows where I got it from." My stomach was tied in knots but I tried to stay calm. "So he doesn't have it?" "He says that he hasn't seen any symptoms."

"What are the symptoms?" She rattled off a list of things and I felt like I had at least two of the long list. Shit, do I have it? "So I just found out right before you came over... so I'm sorry I'm a little bit wound up." I felt like someone punched me in the stomach. Why didn't Clarence tell me? I had a million questions in my head. "Maybe we should wrap gifts another day," I told her, standing up and grabbing my things. "No...I didn't mean to scare you off—I just wanted to tell you the truth." Now she wanted to speak in truths. "Yeah, well, it's cool. You have a lot on your mind. We can do this another day." I started to think of a clinic that could do a walk-in appointment this time of day. I needed to figure out if I had anything... especially before I gave it to Tron. "Well...okay. Maybe tomorrow. You know, Christmas is close, so we need to get these done quick. "Yeah...of course. See you later..." I grabbed my purse, ready to run out, when she grabbed my arm. "Wait, can I get a hug?" Ma had been on this kick since grandma died, wanting to show a lot of affection that I wasn't used to, but I humored her. Wrapping my arms around me for a hug, she even closed her eyes, pulling me close. Meanwhile I just wanted her hands off me. "Did you hear anything about Granny's estate?" I asked her. "Yeah, the lawyer is working on everything. It's going to take a while, maybe even a year." I should have known the old bitch couldn't do right by us, even in death. "Alright...see you later." I darted out of the house to my car, ready to give Clarence a piece of my mind. I tried calling him, but the phone went straight to voicemail. "Hey Clarence. I need to ask you a question about a gift for Mom. Give me a call back...thanks." I sounded polite but there would be no gift for Mom unless we were going to tell her that we were fucking for Christmas. For right now, I needed a doctor—and fast—because if I gave a disease to my fiancé, there was going to be more than some ornaments missing...someone was going to lose their life

"Tron, I'm so glad you could help." Women always said that shit, but this was just about business. Just so happens that I was helping out my mother-in-law. I couldn't hardly classify what I was doing as helping, but I accepted her thank-you anyway as one of my tech guys drilled holes into the wall. "No problem, Yvette. It's really Jose here you should be thanking. I'm just overseeing." We laughed but it was true. When Yvette called and asked me did I know of any good home alarm companies, it was the best time to tell her about our new venture. "I'm just glad I could shoot you some business, son-in-law. So is this with the dealership, or…?" "Naw, this is my business completely separate from that. Gotta keep this money rolling in." And pay off a few things I had going on. "That's great. You are so clever. Have you and Donnie decided on a date yet?" It took me a sec to get on the same page with what she was talking about. "Oh, a wedding date…" "Yeah silly. What else would I be talking about." "My bad, Ms. Yvette. I've been working some crazy hours." Crazy was an understatement. I had damn near been living at the dealership to get things popping. "I admire that work ethic in you. You've bought a new home. You've proposed to my daughter. All this makes you a really upstanding young man." She didn't know me for real, she only knew the person playing this small role in front of her. I considered myself the best actor in the world, so of course she thought I was a good guy. "Thank you. Just trying to build something like what my parents have. They've been married for almost forty years." "Whew, that's a long time. My god." It was hard to fathom, my damn self. "I bet they have been through a lot together." She didn't know the half of it. My father was a pastor and that was probably where I got my acting skills from. He acted every day like he was a faithful man of God, all the while fucking every woman in the church. But somehow my mother stayed true and at his side. Now he was a reformed whore doing whatever she told him. Maybe that's why I showered Donesha with gifts. I didn't deserve her and if she knew the shit I did behind her back, this whole family was going to hate me. "Yeah they've been through it all, but that legacy of love runs in my family. Your daughter is the most important person in my life and I want to be with her forever." I could have been a pastor, I was so good at talking people into things. Just like my dad made the bitches in the church swoon, I was just as good at talking hoes out of their draws. "Well I admire that, and I'm glad to have you as my son-in-law." She gave me a hug, her warm, squishy melons pushing into my chest. "All right...we're all done." Jose hopped down from the ladder, showing her the controls and codes. "All right, here is how you set up your codes and this one camera is over the front porch so you can see what's happening. And here is the rest of the house."

He pushed buttons on the tablet, showing her all of the controls. "I'm going to get those little bastards that keep stealing off my porch. Yesterday they put toilet paper in the trees. Had to hire someone to come get it out." "Who do you think it is?" "Probably kids. The neighborhood is quiet. I can't see anybody else doing it." I didn't say a word, since it wasn't my place to be all in people's shit, but I bet it was a bitch looking for Clarence. "Well, when you figure it out, make sure you tell your neighbors about the business." "Oh definitely." Jose was supposed to be packing up, but he was too busy gawking at Yvette's ass while she talked to me. "Come on Jose, let's get going. We got another appointment coming up." He was all in her ass like a thong, damn near getting caught looking when she turned around. "So, how many cameras is it again?" "We did the six cameras—three outside, then here by the front door inside, one in the kitchen and another in the upstairs balcony. "Perfect, that should give me every angle of the house." "Yep, pretty much." "All right, let me know if you have any issues with it. I can come over and help." "I think I've got it. Basically I can look in with this app on my phones or tablets, right?" "Yep, and if you're in the house you can dial in directly. I left the instructions on the coffee table." "Let me put that up. Clarence will mess around and throw it away. He's always cleaning up and throwing away shit." I didn't say a word, just leaving it all alone, but I knew a hoe-ass nigga when I saw one, and Clarence was it. "Can I talk to you for a second, Tron?" Yvette asked, just as we were about to make it out the door. "Umm yeah, I got a few minutes. Jose, I'll meet you outside." When Jose was finally gone, she let it out. "I know you're working extra hard now and because you're going to be family, I just want to let you know something. Granny Lynn did leave us some money." I felt my heart rate increase when she said that. "Really...Donesha didn't tell me anything about some money." I would have listened to that. At this point, all she was doing was talking about her clients or thinking about how much money she wanted to spend on this lavish wedding she had in mind. "Well, Nene and Lonnie don't know about it yet. I haven't told them. It's a lot of money and I don't want them to blow through it." Blow through it? "Wow...well that's good news." I needed to know how much. This could change everything. "I haven't worked out the final numbers yet, but it looks like we will all receive two hundred and fifty thousand, tax free." I almost collapsed. My legs really did buckle a bit as my mind started flipping through the money. The shit I could do with that type of change! I could get some monkeys off my back and breathe. I managed to keep a calm and even expression on my face as I stared into Yvette's eyes. "Wow, that's a serious amount of money." "Yeah, and my girls are irresponsible with money...well, Donesha is at least. I think Lanesha will be fine." My stomach rumbled hearing her name. I had just quit this bitch, pushed her face into the dirt by proposing to her sister right in her face, and now she was about to get two hundred thousand dollars. "Yeah, you might be right." I needed that money, the shit I could do with that money— hell, they both could give me fifty grand and wouldn't miss it. "So...yeah, that's all on my mind. Then this house situation." "Well...Ma, if I can help you in any way, just let me know." Like holding some of that money, but I would work on that later. "I'm just glad I could tell you. The only people that know are—you, me, and Clarence now—and I want to keep it that way." "Your secret is safe with me." She smiled, looking relieved, but I had more questions. When was this money going to drop? But my cell phone buzzing and Jose staring at Yvette's ass like he was about to jack off right in the front yard, pushed me to leave. "I gotta get to our next appointment. But I'll see you on Christmas, Mom." "Awww, you called me 'Mom.'" She started to blush a little bit and pulled me in for a hug again, her titties in my chest like pillows, but if this was what I had to do to stay good with the family then so be it. "Okay...see you later." Outside I could barely breathe as I damn near ran to the truck. "Damn, your mother-in-law is fine. You know what they say...that's how your girl is going to look in twenty-or-so years." "Man...Stop that shit don't make me think about that." Glancing back up at the house, he could see still her in the window with her head in the tablet. "I'm just saying, bro. That's how it goes. You picked a good bloodline." He laughed, but my mind was on some money. "Yeah man...whatever. I just sent you a text of the next address. Go ahead and get over there and get your gear out. This house is going to need twelve cameras. "Damn…man, you can't laugh." "Not right now, Jose. Got business." The missed called stared back at me…I hadn't spoken to her in a few days and I knew why she was calling. "I got a call. I'm gonna head over there. See you in about thirty minutes." Jumping into the car, I had one thing on my mind now. And that was securing the bag, but first I had to move some shit out of the way. "Hello…this is Tron." "Tron, this is Emily back at the dealership…we have a little situation." "What? A customer? I'll be back there later." "No, not quite…a young lady is here. She said her name is…." I heard a bit of rustling with the phone, and then screams. "My name is Eve, dammit. He knows me. Tell him the mother of his soon-to-be-born child is here." A headache started to pound up the back of my neck. "I'll be right there…I'm on my way." Jumping in the car, I burned rubber all the way back to the dealership. My fucking life depended on stopping this bitch from letting the cat out of the bag before she ruined it. There were police cars everywhere, and pieces of paper flying through the air. I picked one up as I got out of the car, and felt like my whole life had ended. The flyer read, "Trontavious Carter fucks his customers and takes advantage of them to sell cars," and a bunch of other shit, but it was all I could read before I heard her voice. "There he is, little bastard...how you gonna deny me and my baby?" she screamed, as the police tried to get her to calm down. "Sir, do you know this woman?" the officer asked, approaching me with one of the flyers in his hand. "Yes sir." "She has been disturbing the premises and claims to want to speak with you. Do you want to speak to her?" I wouldn't spit on the bitch if she was on fire. "No sir. I know her, but she is trespassing. "Trespassing my ass, you bastard..." "Eve...I need you to leave now." I tried to keep smiling as people looked at us through the dealership windows. This was creating a scene. I saw customers driving off, others avoiding the lot all together, and up towards the door was my boss looking down. "EVE... EVE... GET THE FUCK OUT OF HERE, MAN!!" The cops instantly went for their guns, their hands hovering over their revolvers like they were going to shoot me. "Sir, we need you to calm down. There is no need to yell." But this bitch wasn't at their job tripping, she was at mine in the middle of the day, acting like a complete ass out here for these people. "Stop fucking playing, Tron—you aren't going to shovel me and my baby under no fucking..." She doubled over, holding her stomach. "Officer...she is trespassing; can you make her leave?" "Oh my god...call an ambulance!" "I haven't fucking touched you. I'm over here...stop with this." "Sir, can you maybe get in your vehicle..." "I work here. I'm going inside to work." "Oh my god...help me...my baby... my stomach..." She was down on her knees now, holding her stomach like something was really bothering her. "I'm going inside. Come get me if you need me." I walked off, leaving her and the police behind, but the hell in front of me was way worse. "Carter...what did I just tell you?" "Sir, look...it isn't my fault...I didn't ask her..." "You're fired." He said it so easy that I barely thought he was serious. "What?" "You're fucking fired. I can't have this. Your numbers have been low anyway. Clear out your desk. I'll have payroll send your check." I was stuck to the ground and couldn't move until I heard the sirens. Turning around, I saw there was now an ambulance on the lot. Eve was being put on a gurney and put into the back of an ambulance. The bitch had really put on a fucking show and now I didn't have a job. "Sir, I…" But he was going. I turned around to see my boss—or ex-boss—,was already inside far away from me. It felt like I was floating in the air watching myself, as I felt my body turn hot as a volcano. "FUCK THIS!" I was inside the dealership, yelling at my boss, but he wouldn't turn around. "Go home, Tron…it's over." "But I built this, motherfucker…I was here when you had nobody." He still wouldn't even give the decency to look at me. Instead I saw him motion to the security guard. After all this time, the motherfuckers were trying to throw me out. With the strength of Mike Tyson, I picked up a chair and threw it as hard as I could at one of the glass windows. Instantly, the huge twelve-foot window shattered, sending people running and screaming for cover. Of course this sent the police who were still in the parking lot, running towards me with their guns out. I heard, "FREEZE...GET DOWN ON THE GROUND." Their guns were drawn and pointed on me as the whole staff and customers ducked for cover. This wasn't supposed to happen; it was supposed to be a good day. Now here in my good suit, I was kneeling down in shattered glass pieces as the cops jumped on me. In the very place where I had closed hundreds of thousands of dollars' worth of deals, I was now getting handcuffed and dragged out like a criminal. All because of some pussy.

Chapter Eleven

LANESHA

"You have a collect call from…" I knew it had to be a wrong number. I didn't know a damn soul that would call me collect. "Trontavius Carter." I couldn't believe my ears. What the hell was he calling me for? I sat up in bed fast, pressing "one" quick, before they could hang up. "Go ahead with your call." I heard the operator, and seconds later, his voice. "Lonnie…" "Tron...what the hell is going on?" "I fucked up...I fucked up really bad." I didn't know what that meant, but as he talked I was already getting dressed. "Where are you?" I asked, pulling on sweatpants. Wherever he was, I was going to get him—that was no question. "Downtown at the jail...my bond is two thousand. I can get it back to you as soon as…" "Tron, I already know you will. Just tell me what I need to do." He gave me the instructions and I was out of the house in seconds. First to the ATM, and then downtown in the middle of rush-hour traffic. I battled through it all to get to this man that I loved. I don't know why I loved him—it wasn't my intention. Even though I was mad at him, I still dropped everything as soon as I heard he needed me. Through metal detectors at the jail I went, then paid the bond. I could have left and let him find his own way home, but my heart wouldn't let me move until he was free. The sun went down and there I was, in my car waiting and watching the back door where the prisoners were released. Finally around eight o'clock, I saw him come out the doors looking like he had lost his entire soul. "Tron, over here…" I yelled to him, waving my hands. He picked up his step, damn near running to the car and jumping in like someone was chasing him. "Baby, you ok?" Shit...I didn't mean to call him that. "I mean,

Tron…" "I fucked up. I've fucked up completely." "What happened?" "I don't want to talk about it. I just…I need to go get my car. Take me to the dealership please…" "Your job." "My old job." I didn't know what he meant by his "old job." "What old job?" "I got fired, okay…from the dealership, for a stupid-ass reason. Please can you just take me there—I don't want to talk right this second." I did as he said, pulling off the curb and not saying a single word. For the entire drive we rode in silence until arriving at the dealership. Looking up at the huge building, the thing that stuck out to me was a boarded up window. Plywood covered where glass used to be, and I wanted to ask a million questions but I didn't say a word. Instead I pulled next to his car and parked, waiting for him to get out. "Look, thank you for coming to get me," he finally said. "I'll get your money back to you tomorrow when the bank opens." I knew that already. He was too proud to let me give him money, but the bigger question to me was "why. " "Why didn't you call your fiancé?" I asked the question that was burning in my head since I heard he was in jail. "Because. She'll have a million questions and I don't want to answer them right now. Besides, she's at her labs for school tonight. She turns her phone off and leaves it in the car, so she wouldn't have been any help." "So it's me you depend on. You shit on me and propose to her but it's me you want to act like your fucking wife." "Calm down…" "No, you calm down. That bitch isn't who you think she is, yet I'm here helping you…" Before I could finish, his lips were on mine, his tongue exploring my mouth as he pulled me close. I hadn't been hugged, touched, or kissed since the last time I was with him and I didn't realize how lonely I was. How I longed for his touch, and now that we were here together, my anger seemed to dissolve away. "I'm sorry…I fucked up so much and today was like the grand finale." he began. "I did wrong and I want to fix it. You mind if I come over to your place? We can talk about it." Talk? We never talked when he came over to my house. It was always non-stop fuck sessions and as bad as I wanted to hold my ground, I could only tell him one thing. "Yes…"

Chapter Twelve

DONESHA

I haven't been able to sleep or eat since my sister found me and Clarence in my kitchen. When I first started with Clarence, I told myself it was revenge, that I hoped my mom found out one day and felt as much pain as I did. But when I saw Lanesha glaring down at us, all I could feel was shame—I didn't my mama to find out. I was pissed at her, angry about so many things, but the last thing I wanted was her to find out I was fucking her husband. It was wrong and fucked up. That's why I was here at her house to straighten everything out. I knew she was gone for the night, Work meetings, late night shopping, and her book club would have her away from the house until midnight. Meanwhile Tron was at work and I was supposed to be at school. This was the perfect time for me to get away and tell Clarence face-to-face that we were through. Standing on the front porch, I took a deep breath before knocking, but he opened the door before I had the chance. "Hello…" He even talked seductive when he greeted me. I could feel his eyes feasting on my body as I walked in, but I wasn't here for that. "We need to talk." "Okay…have a seat…" "No…I'm going to stand right here by the door." "Can I at least close it?" It seemed silly to have the front door wide open while we talked. "Yeah, of course." I moved so he could shut it, his cologne wafting past my nostrils as he brushed past me. "Okay…so what's on your mind?" "I can't do this anymore. I thought that was clear when Tron proposed to me…" Clarence laughed as the words came out. "That chump. He ain't no real man, so why would I take that shit seriously?" "Because it's my life, Clarence. You can't hold me hostage in this lie until you decide to leave my mother. We've been screwing around for too long." "Why can't shit stay the way that it is for now? I told you I'm trying to work some things out. I can't just move when you want me to move." "Well you can't pop up at my house trying to fuck me. What if that would have been Tron instead of Lanesha." He didn't say a word, instead he took a step closer to me. "You think I'm afraid of him." "I...I don't know." He stepped another foot closer as I stepped back, until my back was against the door. "Well, I'm not. I'm a grown man, I will never be afraid of a little boy." "But...he's my fiancé..." "That's fine. I got a wife but I'm in love with you." I heard the words, letting them sit in my brain for a moment. He was only a few inches in front of me now. "I...I just can't do this anymore." "Is it that you can't, you won't, or you're afraid?" I didn't know how to answer that question and sometimes I felt all of those emotions and a million more. But right now I wanted to stay strong; I had to break this cycle. "Look I..." His lips covered mine before another word could get out. He pulled open my jacket, damn near yanking it off me, and as strong as I thought I was before I stepped into this house, I was powerless against him. Clarence was right, he was a man that knew what he wanted. Tron never handled me like this or acted like he wanted me. But on the other end, Clarence acted like a ravenous lion, pouncing on me and pulling me close like he couldn't live without me. "I love you…" He said it over and over as he kissed down my neck. Tugging at my sweater, it was off in seconds and thrown to the floor. One by one he pulled my breasts from the bra until eventually that was pulled over my head too. My nipples in his mouth, he toyed, tongued and played with them until I moaned his name. "This is your pussy." He told me, grabbing the crotch area of my jeans. "I know how to make it cum and only I can make it cum," he told me as he pulled down my pants. He knelt down, eye-level with my pussy, breathing hot air through my panties and making me squirm and pant for him. My eyes searched over the room. Seeing a picture of him with my mother in her wedding gown stopped my excitement for a moment. I was ready to tell him to stop, when I felt his tongue push my panties to the side. Draping one leg over his shoulder, his face was right between my legs, licking me like a dehydrated dog at a water bowl. He gulped me up while putting feather-light kisses on my clit that turned into hard sucks. I closed my eyes so I couldn't see her looking at me. I closed my eyes and blocked out everything but the intense pleasurable pain below my waist as my body began to shake. "Yeah... cum for daddy...cum for me," he begged, and I couldn't say no. He knew my body, he knew what made me tick and as he licked some more I became puddy-pinned to the door. I came, legs shaking and weak as he rose to his feet. His pants at his ankles, and my mind delirious from his tongue lashing, he entered me. I thought for a moment about a condom, how my mom told me she had an STD, but right now my pussy didn't care. He entered me hard, filling my pussy to capacity as I held on. He picked me up, hoisting me up with my back pinned against the door and my legs wrapped around his waist. "I love you...I.fucking.love.you.girl," he told me over and over, pushing into me, knocking aside every piece of guilt I thought I felt. My eyes peeled open for a moment, seeing my mother look at me in her white wedding dress. I imagined her crying, pleading, begging me not to hurt her. But in her house, in her living room, I let her husband fuck me. As I screamed his name and clawed at his back I felt nothing but pleasure. Shame was on the floor, probably near my bra and discarded clothes. As long as Clarence kept giving me dick like this, I couldn't pinpoint me ever being able to tell him no.

Chapter Thirteen

CLARENCE

The living room smelled like passion when we were done. She left without a word, grabbing her clothes, then dressed quietly and slipped out the door just as quickly as she came. I knew what she felt—probably guilt and pain about what we were doing—but that was life. Life was pain, and I wasn't about to deny myself some pleasure just because of our situations. "We can have it both ways...no one has to know," I told her before she left, but she still didn't' say a word. "I watched her drive off and then I went into cleanup mode—airing the house out, vacuuming the living room and even cleaning rooms that we didn't even go in. Just in case my wife came home with an ultrasonic nose and a hint of female intuition, I was going to be ready for anything. I even cooked dinner, then waited and waited, but I must have dozed off in my man cave. I woke up to my wife shaking me awake. "Baby...it's time to get up." "Damn...how long was I asleep? You didn't wake me up." "No, you looked so peaceful. I called your name and you didn't move, so I decided to just let you stay there." That was a good move; I had the best sleep of my life in here. And if she didn't wake me up, that meant only one thing. Yvette had no idea I fucked the shit out of her daughter in the foyer last night. "Well, let me get up and get to work. Did you pack my bags for my business trip?" "I sure did. Everything is packed and waiting by the stairs." "You're the best, boo. Thank you for that." I gave her a kiss on the cheek. Making my way to the bathroom, she started her normal morning ritual of talking my fucking head off. "So last night at the book club, Gina didn't even read the book and kept interrupting everybody." I pretended to listen, going through the motions of hearing all about her bullshit as I tried to take a morning shower. As she rambled and I pretended to care, I thought about Donesha last night. How it felt to feel her cum in my face. How pushing my dick inside her wetness felt like heaven on earth wrapped around my dick. I wanted her now. I wished she was here with me and I would take her right in the shower. Just thinking about it had my dick hard. Taking advantage of all the soap suds and warm water, I gripped my tool as Yvette rambled on while applying her makeup. "And then I get home and I see that the damn kids stole my fucking miniature lawn Santa again." She was always rambling about those damn lawn items. "That's crazy…" I squeezed my dick, imagining Donesha's small Milk Dud breasts on my tongue. "Yeah, it's okay though, I'll just roll back the cameras." Everything in my body went cold. My dick seemed to instantly go limp, and within seconds was drooping down to the floor. "What cameras?" "Remember I told you I was going to get the alarm." "Yeah…" "Well, with the alarm comes cameras." "Wait a minute...you put cameras on my house and didn't tell me?" I was beyond pissed, yanking back the shower curtain to get a full look at her. "Yeah, I didn't' get a chance to tell you. When Tron came over to show…" "Tron…what the hell was he doing here?" She looked at me as if I had three heads. "Clarence—why are you getting so angry? Let me finish and you'll get the damn answers." "Fine, tell me now." "Tron has a new company working with an home alarm company and…" I didn't want to hear shit about what he had. "Spare me the details. Why was he here." "He got me a discount on the alarm and was here when the installer came. Jeez, what the hell is wrong with you?" "What about these cameras? Where are they?" "Outside the house, and one at the front door, and the side kitchen door and…" "Jesus Christ, Yvette, you have fucking people watching my house and you don't let me know. I was in my boxers, walking around the house free." I grabbed a towel as I stepped out to face her. "Not anyone. It's recording, but only we can access." "Then how…how do I access it?" "I don't know. I have to call Tron and figure it out. He told me how to do it, but with all that shit at the book club last night I can't remember." She laughed, reaching out to touch me, but this wasn't funny to me. "No...I'm mad that you don't communicate with me." "I told you I was doing it. I even left the code for you." "I knew about the alarm but I didn't' know about no damn cameras, Yvette...you better stop doing shit without consulting me." "Wow...I didn't' know you were my damn daddy." I stared her down and before I knew it, the itch in my hand couldn't be denied. I swung my open hand and connected right with her face. "Bitch, don't you get smart with me. What I tell you about your smart-ass mouth...huh?" We'd had this problem a dozen times, but when I stopped putting my foot up her ass a few months ago, I thought we were past this. Now I saw that a good ass-kicking was what she needed. She scrambled away, pushing herself across the huge bathroom to a corner furthest away from me. "You said you would never hit me again." "You said you would tell me shit and communicate. I guess we both fucked up." I glared at her, putting the fear of God into her. "Get me access to those damn cameras today. And don't do shit-else in MY house without asking." I left her there in the bathroom crying. I got dressed in a flash, not caring about where she was, but instead I was down in the living room staring face-to-face at a small, flashing red light. Right over the door, pointed directly down, was this camera. "I'm gone…" I yelled upstairs, grabbing my keys and my phone. I had to get out of the house. I couldn't stay there for another second. Out in my car, before I even left the driveway, I made a call. She didn't answer. I expected that, but she had to be warned. "Nene…it's Clarence. We have a problem. Call me back," I told her, not wanting to say too much over the phone. Hopefully that slap and my anger would keep Yvette rattled enough to not look at the cameras. If she did, I was as good as fucked.

Chapter Fourteen
YVETTE

He said he would never hit me again. A promise he made after months of therapy and begging me to stay. "I promise I'll never do it again. I'm better now, I promise." He promised and I believed him, gave him the benefit of the doubt on many things. Now I was sitting in my living room with a swollen face. The moment he got angry, I knew there must be something on the camera. "A man will tell on himself every time." Even though my Mama was horrible at listen to her own advice she was always spot on. A man will get angry when their caught and Clarence got more than angry, he was down right in a rage and I needed to know why. I called off from work, then sat on the couch and watched the feed from all the cameras. And what I saw damn near sent me into a rage. I watched as my husband, caressed and fucked another woman. I watched as she enjoyed him, and screamed his name. And then, seeing the face of the child I brought into this world basically stabbed me in the heart. I watched her, as I heard her screams through the microphone in the camera. I heard him tell her that he loved her and then I watched as they departed and he cleaned up the house like nothing happened. I sat on the couch watching the clip all day crying, then throwing things, but then my brain cleared. Everything that was fuzzy became laser focused for me and I realized one thing. My daughter really hates me. Whatever I did to her scarred her so bad that she could do something like this. And my husband. The bastard was a cheater, a manipulator, and an abuser but this was an all-time low. I ran upstairs to pack my things. He was away on a trip and by the time he made it back I would be gone. But how far would I get? I grabbed my shoes calculating how much money I had, and it was barely twenty dollars in my purse. The most I could take out of our bank account was two hundred dollars without it triggering a notification that went straight to Clarence's phone. My inheritance wasn't final. The money was frozen in an account that I couldn't touch until everything was clear. I stood in my huge bedroom surrounded by suitcases with nowhere to go. I couldn't leave, not yet anyways. I turned off my heart and turned on my mind, thinking of exactly how to get out of this and get everyone back that wronged me. Finding my secret stash of cigarettes and a tall glass of wine, I drank and smoked for hours until I came up with the right solution. When I did, I made a call and waited for my doorbell to ring. I cleaned myself up, changed clothes, and covered my swollen face the best I could under makeup before he showed up at my door. "Ms. Yvette, what's going on?" Tron stood at my door, smiling from ear to ear with a set of tools in his hand. "Well, it looks like my husband doesn't want cameras in his house. So I was wondering if you could take them down." I called him after I stopped crying. When I figured out I couldn't leave, I had to be smart. This was a part of me being smart. "Oh...okay no problem." he came in but I could tell something was bothering him. Maybe he knew that my daughter was a slut already, but there was no way he could step foot in this house and know it was Clarence. Just thinking about it made my bones shudder. "What's wrong, son? Come sit down and talk to me." "It's nothing...just a lot of stress on my mind." "Well, tell you what. Why don't I get you a drink and you tell me all about it." He accepted, and I went right to Clarence's Hennessy Black, the good shit that costs hundreds a bottle. I didn't give a damn about him complaining about me serving it to guests. Maybe he would hit me for that too, but right now I didn't care. Instead, I poured my son-in-law a big glass. "Here you go. Now tell me all about it." He sipped the Hennessy and told me that he got fired. "It was some misunderstanding at the job. Shit got crazy. I broke a glass window, then they arrested me." "Jesus, Tron. That is too much." "I know...I haven't even told Nene yet." Fuck that bitch. I didn't care if she lived or died anymore. To me she was already dead. "Well, don't worry 'bout a thing. I'll make sure to shoot you some business on the alarm side. There are a few neighbors that would probably want alarms when I introduce that at the homeowners meeting." "Really...that would help a lot. Thank you." he smiled for the first time since he got here. Sipping his drink, he talked about random shit like the weather, but my eyes were on his pants. The best revenge is the one you don't expect, I thought to myself as I watched his lips, wondering how good it would feel to have his mouth on my pussy. I had changed my ways, reformed, went to church, got a good husband, and now I get repaid for all of that hard work by being disrespected by not only my daughter but my husband. And now, I'm sitting in front of my daughter's most prized possession, her man. "Well, let me get to work on taking these cameras down." He went to stand but I grabbed his hand, pulling him back down into the couch. "Sit and enjoy your drink." "What about Clarence? I know he doesn't like me for real." Tron laughed. "If he came in here and saw us drinking, he..."

"Don't worry about him. He's gone for the weekend on a business trip." I couldn't stop staring at his lips. They looked so luscious the way he licked them. His clear face with not one blemish, and his hair so long and dreaded, he looked like a lion sitting in front of me. "Oh, okay…" He seemed to relax a little bit. "You know…I wonder, is my daughter treating you right." "What do you mean?" "Well, when you have a man for a long time you become complacent." I looked at his drink, it was half gone and he was smiling from ear to ear as I spoke. It was official. He was drunk enough for what I needed to do. "Shit is hard with her…oops I mean, stuff." He smiled, giggling. "It's okay baby, you're grown. I'm grown too. And from now on I don't want you to call me "Ms. Yvette"…just call me Yvette, alright?" "Okay…Yvette…" "I'm not that old. You know I was fifteen when I had the girls. I just turned forty." "I know. That's crazy because you look the same age as them. Hell you might look younger than the girls." I smiled at that as I scooted a little closer to him, my hand resting on his shoulder. "Well yeah, you see I'm still young." He laughed. "You look so tense. Let me give you a massage." Standing up in front of him with my breasts damn near in his face, I began to massage. From his shoulders and neck, I moved to his chest and arms. "Oh, you're so tight...what else is tight on you?" He laughed. "You know, I appreciate this, but…" "Nonsense...let me finish. Lie back on the couch." "But…" "Just do it... what—are you scared of me?" He didn't say a word. Still smiling, he lied back on the couch. He closed his eyes as I continued to massage down his chest and the chiseled stomach I could feel through his shirt. As I got to his pants, unbuckling his belt was easy, and he didn't move to stop me until I had his zipper all the way down. "Wait... what are you doing?" I didn't answer. Instead, I pulled his already-hard dick out of his pants. It pointed straight up to the ceiling as if it was saying "Hi." "I'm just massaging you baby." Before he could object, I slide his dick in my mouth, sucking him down my throat with every muscle of my body. I started slow, speeding up and slopping my spit on his dick as he moaned. "We shouldn't...you shouldn't do….ahhhh….ohhhh shit…"

He couldn't resist, my head was irresistible to any man, and this little boy whose dick I had in my jaws was no match. But I wanted more than his dick in my mouth. After Donesha fucked my husband in my house, it was only right that I give her fiancé a try. His dick was bigger than I thought. It was a challenge getting him all inside my throat, but I did it, swallowing every bit of him until I felt his hot cum filling my mouth. I swallowed, something I would have never done for Clarence, but if he wanted to go down on people why shouldn't I? "Damn, Yvette...fuck I can't believe…" he was in shock, stuck on the couch as I rose to my feet and took off my clothes. "I want you to fuck me...fuck me like you do my daughter... No...NO...I want you to fuck me better than that. Do you hear me?" "Yes…" "Yes, what?" He looked confused, like he wasn't sure what to say. A stiff slap to his face sent a jolt through him. "I said, "Yes, What?" I growled as I pulled off my shirt. "Yes Ma'am…" "With a smile and a now-naked body, I eased down on this young boy with the dick like a horse and the abs of an Olympic sprinter. "I want you to make me cum...you think you can do that?" I asked, as he was now completely inside me. Riding him slow, I looked him right in the eye. "Come on can't you fuck...or you just lie there and get fucked like a little bitch. I thought you were a man?" With men, their pride was always deep. And after getting slapped and made to say "Yes Ma'am, I knew it wouldn't be long before the beast in him came out. With the rage of a young bull, he pulled off his shirt and grabbed my hair. He thrust his dick into me as he pushed me down harder. "You wanna get fucked...I'll fuck you," he said, flipping me over, pulling his pants off the rest of the way and getting on top. Chest to chest, eye to eye, he pushed his dick back inside of me so deep I thought he had broken something. What I felt was an explosion of pleasure as he grinded his hips into me. "Say my name bitch..." he grabbed my hair, pulling it with every thrust. "Tron... Tron...Oh Tron, fuck me!" I begged and pleaded. I imagined my daughter seeing this; I thought of the terror that would be in her eyes. Whatever hate she thought she felt toward my mother would be nowhere near what she was going to feel for me. And the pain that Clarence caused would be nothing compared to the humiliation I was about to unleash on his life. They both had messed with the wrong person. I'm Corrine Hollins' child, one of the baddest bitches in the Midwest, and now it was time for me to show my true colors.

Chapter Fifteen

BRYAN

Holidays were his busiest time of year and he loved every minute of it. Even now, cleaning up his 'workspace,' as he liked to call it, of any blood was more like a scavenger hunt than real work. Dressed in all black from his black skull cap and gloves all the way down to his black boots, the man was on a mission to finish his job with the precision and care that he was known for. In the pitch dark room he shined the black light across the floor looking for any blood or bodily fluids. "Come on...I know something is out there," he grumbled. Finally, in the corner by the door, he found it - one single drop of blood. Spraying a bleach solution he cleaned the lone piece of evidence and turned the lights back on. Stuffing the tools of his trade back into a black satchel bag that hung off his shoulder, he looked over his work. His target sat slumped over her desk, a mid-forties, blonde-haired marketing executive now dead from two gunshot wounds to the head. It was his best work, but she did put up a bit of a fight, hence the need to check the 'workspace' for any blood particles. He made sure to open a window, letting in the cold air and letting out the full stench of evacuated bodily fluids from his latest kill. "Alright. Looks like I'm all clear," he whispered to himself, shutting off the light again and walking briskly out the office door. Down the hallway and to the steps the athletically built man - tall enough to be a star basketball player - seemed to zoom down the ten flights to the first floor. At the bottom, he calmed himself, steadied his breathing, and just as he was about to go outside his phone rang. "Shit…" He jumped slightly, startled by the phone but the name on the screen wouldn't allow him to ignore it. Family first was always the motto so he answered the phone and entered the cold darkness of night. "Hey Clarence...wassup bruh? Where you at? Sounds noisy," Bryan observed as he entered a dark alley towards a busy street where he could get lost in a crowd. Just before he made it to the road, he carefully took out the weapon he'd used tonight and threw it in a sewer grate. He was almost thankful for the cold; gloved hands eliminated fingerprints but they were more suspicious in warm weather. "I'm in an airport. One last trip before the end of the year...you know the hustle doesn't stop." Clarence laughed and so did Bryan "You're preaching to the choir, fam. I'm on the job right now." "Bryan my brother always working and getting his paper. I'm proud of you bruh." They talked to each other like close brothers but they were more like brothers from a different mother. Step siblings from a relationship that hadn't lasted, the men still called each other brother, especially when one of them needed something. "Oh...just working. You know how that goes." Bryan downplayed the situation as he walked through the streets, blending in with the rest of the holiday shoppers in the downtown shopping district. Everyone was so busy getting out of the cold that no one noticed the man dressed in black from head to toe walking through the crowd. He slipped anonymously through the crowd, all of them oblivious to the fact that he had a gun big enough to kill an elephant on his right hip. "Yeah I feel you bruh. You coming over for our New Year's celebration?" Clarence asked. Bryan thought about it as he made it to his all Black CLS Benz, parked a comfortable seven blocks from his target. "Umm...I don't know about that." Bryan surveyed his surroundings making sure he wasn't followed before jumping in the fine German engineering and taking off. "Come on bruh I need a favor from you." "A favor?" "Is this line secure?" Clarence asked before he continued. "Negative...I will need a second line for that. You know that number." Before Bryan could get the sentence out, his second phone began to ring from the cup holder. "Yeah?" he answered "This is secure right?" Clarence asked urgently. "Yep...wassup." "I got a dilemma I need you to handle." "Like what?" Bryan was down for anything from kidnapping to outright murder; he was what some would call a hit man but he preferred being called a problem solver. "I need you to take care of something for me but… it's a little different. You remember my daughter-in law-right?" Bryan thought quickly as he started the car and slowly left the curb. "Which one?" "The younger one…" Bryan had a damn near photographic memory, he could remember anything and could immediately picture the woman in question. "Lanesha, right?" "Yeah that's the one. I need you to…befriend her and get something back for me." "Ahh, like that one chick in college you had me 'befriend' so you could get a better grade." Clarence laughed at that. Sometimes he forgot about all of their dealings together, some vanilla and some much worse. "Yeah something like that. And she's going to be at the party so…" "Say no more," Bryan answered. "Send me a picture and her info. I'll figure it out." "Aww thanks, bruh. I really appreciate it." "What is this about anyway?" Bryan asked, relaxing a little as he left the shopping district far behind him, along with the skyscraper where his latest victim was slumped over a desk. She wouldn't probably be found until morning and by then he would be so far removed from the area, no one would know where to start with clues. "I got caught up fam…" Clarence hedged. "Be specific." Bryan asked as he shot onto the highway. Merging onto the three lane expressway then shooting past cars like a slingshot in his all black, luxury getaway car. Clarence explained the situation and Bryan listened, filing information into his mind like the human filing cabinet that he was. "So I need you to get close to her. See if you can calm this situation down and maybe if she has companionship then… "Then she won't blow the whistle on you," Bryan said connecting the dots. "Exactly!" Giving his head a small rub he made a quick decision. "Fine…I'll be there." "My brother…thanks fam." "This should square us up on that one situation right?" Bryan hated owing people and he paid back all of his debts but the one he owed his step-brother Clarence was one of his biggest. "Yep, this will make us completely square. You keep her quiet and I'm good." "No dirt naps?" "Nooo…no…not yet at least." Clarence laughed but Bryan found nothing funny. He was completely serious. Killing someone wasn't a laughing matter to Bryan, but he didn't say a word. Instead he just drove, listening to his brother babble for a few minutes. "Alright bruh so I'll see you at my house on New Year's Eve." Clarence finally wound down his steady rant. "Yeah...I'll be there," Bryan said, giving his word and his word was his bond. Rubbing his stubbled chin he thought about what it would take to seduce a woman. He pictured Lanesha, the way she looked the last time he saw her, and he already knew what he had to do. "Alright. See you soon bruh." He had about a week to get ready for his seduction and as he hung up the phone Bryan was already thinking about what he would say. He was the consummate professional and he was unwilling to leave any job to chance, especially when on the job for his family. He would take this just as seriously as a murder-for-hire gig and that meant extensive preparation. Steering with his left hand he used his right to type Lanesha's name into his phone. Using a special database her address, phone number, and recent social media pictures came up. He now had intel on his latest job, and with that information he was sure to have perfect aim and not miss his target..

Chapter Sixteen

YVETTE

s we lay on the living room floor, me smoking a cigarette and Tron staring at the ceiling, I tried to understand why my daughter would give up all of this for old ass Clarence. Clarence whose signature sex move was getting on top every once in a while. But what I saw him doing on that video wasn't the Clarence I knew. He doesn't do shit like that for me. I cried at first and then I got jealous, hate rising up in me til it was in my brain sending me signals to do something. Now, here I was, resting from the aftermath of my decision. "I guess I should get these cameras down...I gotta get out of here," Tron said as he got up. "What's the rush?" I sat up, watching him fumble to get dressed. "I still got some work to do...and Clarence...Donesha... fuck!" He jumped up as if he had just now realized what we were doing. "I can't believe I did this shit." Shit? My pussy was far from shit, it was gold wrapped in a small package. "But you liked it right?" I asked. He didn't speak at first, instead searching for his jeans, pulling them up over his stained boxers. A DNA test would confirm that my pussy juices and his cum were mixed in to form a beautiful artistic pattern of cum stains on his boxers. "Did you hear me?" "Huh?" "You liked right?" I repeated. He thought for a moment, a small smile starting to crease his lips before he started to shake his head. "Don't shake it off, just admit that you liked this pussy." "Yeah it was good but I'm engaged to your daughter. You're married. We shouldn't have done this." He found his shoes and I watched as he finished getting dressed. Then he found the small stepladder and used it to take down the cameras that were inside the house. It seemed to only take him seconds but when he was done he stood by the door like a little puppy waiting for orders. "Are you leaving?" I asked, disappointed. "Yeah I need to go. But I think we need to figure out right now what this is." I went to him, my naked body fully exposed as I pinned him to the wall. "This is whatever the fuck we want it to be." My lips on his and he didn't move away when I put my hands back into his jeans. "This is my dick now. So when I call...you better come running. Understood?" He stared at me, checking my seriousness but there were no smiles or laughs on my face. This was real life and now that I've let him get a taste he belonged to me, no matter who was in the way. "I hear you but, Yvette, we can't do this. This one time was a mistake and…" He kept going but his lips looked so succulent and pink and all I could see was the look he'd had in his eyes as I pushed his face down between my legs. Now he was standing here talking to me with these lips that had my pussy juices glazed all over them only an hour ago. There was no way he would take that away from me no matter what he said. He belonged to me or else. "You get that...or I'll have to let my daughter see what happened here today," I threatened. "What?" It wasn't hard to bring up the footage of our sexcapade up on the security app. I watched as he held on to my phone speechless, his head shaking more with every position that we moved in until I pulled my phone away from his grasp. "Now this is how we are going to play this. I will call you...and you come running when I say. Got it?" It was a take it or leave it proposition and he had no choice. "Fine...whatever...I just can't believe this shit," he said, rubbing his temples like he was trying to push a migraine away. I wanted to tell him how much I enjoyed my time, and how we could make beautiful love together but my phone rang, stealing the moment. My husband's name appeared across the screen and sucked the joy out of the room. "I have to go…" Tron didn't wait for my permission. He was out the door, running to his car like a ghost was chasing him. "Hello…" I answered the phone with a smile on my face. "Baby I'm sorry for what I did," Clarence blurted out as soon as he heard my voice. I listened to him beg and plead through the phone about how he didn't mean it but was he apologizing for hitting me or fucking my daughter? "I don't know what came over me. Maybe I need to go back to counseling or something...I'm so sorry," he went on. I didn't say a word, just holding the phone listening to his sorry excuses. I wondered how long he and Donehsha had been going on. I thought about all the possible signs and I saw nothing. They hated each other. But now I knew that was an act, nothing was true and everyone in my life was fake. My daughter betrayed me and my husband helped her do it. "Baby do you hear me?" I snapped out of my trance to see that Tron's car was gone and Clarence was still on my line babbling. "Yes I hear you, Clarence. I'm getting tired I need to get some rest." "I'll be home tomorrow, beautiful. Maybe we can talk then." I could have left him now, gotten a divorce and submitted the video of him cheating on me as evidence but I wouldn't get my full pay out. Per the prenuptial agreement I would get almost nothing, even if he cheated. Just a little while longer...play the game for a little while, I told myself. I had a plan but it wasn't for the weak and I could play this game better than anybody. "I love you Yvette and I'm sorry..." "I know you do baby. It's okay..." "Really?" I wanted to laugh at his excitement. Hell no it wasn't okay that he hit me but I let him think it was. "Maybe when I get back we can try for a baby one last time." I wanted to laugh at that too. Clarence always wanted to talk about kids. Even though my uterus was closed and would probably be going through menopause soon, I said whatever I could to keep him at ease. No use in spoiling my big reveal before everything was in place. "Yeah maybe we can try one last time this year," I cooed. For a man that was fucking my daughter you would think he would want as little to do with me as possible, but here he was begging me to have a baby. I wonder what he's telling Donesha. "You have no idea how good it feels to hear you say that. I love you baby. I'm all yours for the holidays all the way through the new year." I rolled my eyes at that. I didn't want to be around him non-stop. He had no idea how good it felt to fuck a real man half my age and now I was addicted. But the more my husband thought we were on good terms, the better. Revenge is best served cold anyways.

Every hall, floor, nook, and cranny of Homer Seales Regional Hospital was engraved in Eve's brain. She had walked the halls throughout each night for the past few weeks, to move around and clear her mind. Anything to take her mind off her tiny infant who was fighting for her life. Taking the elevator up to the NICU, Eve went about her normal routine. Smiling and saying hi to all the other parents and nurses that were crowded outside the sterilized room. They all seemed to stare at her and Eve pretended not to notice, but everyone knew that today was the last day. Her angel was going home. She hung up her belongings and began the fifteen minute procedure of scrubbing every particle of dirt and bacteria from her hands. An aid appeared, helping her put on scrubs, head cap, and a mask. Soon she looked like a hazmat worker, covered in yellow with white latex gloves on her hands. "You ready?" the woman asked, but Eve would never be ready for what she had to do. Instead of crying and prolonging the inevitable she simply nodded her head, unable to talk for fear the tears would start flowing. The sounds of machines buzzing and the faint swoosh of ventilators was the soundtrack of the NICU. Eve stepped slowly over to the miniature heated dome that was what her daughter had known as home since the premature delivery. Usually the tiny dome would be dark, filled with tubes, tape, and gauze. But today the lights were on and her little baby was no longer attached to machines but instead dressed and peaceful in a small pink dress. No more cords, tubes, or ventilators were in the way, just a tiny baby with her eyes closed, like a small princess taken away before she could begin. "She looks like she's just sleeping," Eve said from behind her hospital issued mask. Six weeks and her baby girl fought a good fight but now she was resting for eternity with the angels, up in the stars. Today she had finally been called home. "You know her dad didn't come see her...not once." Eve's her voice cracked as she spoke to baby Neveah's nurse. "I named her Neveah because it was Heaven spelled backwards. Now she's in Heaven and he never got to meet her. He didn't come, not even when I told him that this would be happening." Eve wanted to cry, she felt the aching in her eye sockets and intense weight on her chest but no more words would come out. "Yeah she looks peaceful. We got her dressed up for you just like you asked. The priest should be on his way soon," the nurse told her, but there was no need. She just wanted to be alone with her daughter. "Do you want to hold her one last time?" the nurse asked. She wasn't sure if it was healthy to hold her baby's dead body but this would be the only time she would hold the small child without the interference of tubes and machines. "Sure..." Eve sat down in the rocking chair as the nurse placed the peacefully deceased angel in her arms. She had grown a bit since she was born but not enough. There had been too many complications following a risky surgery due to an infection. A week ago the doctors told her there was nothing else they could do. Baby Neveah had fought all she could, but the time was drawing near. "She looks really pretty in this outfit," Eve said as she traced her fingers over the preemie clothes. Neveah was so small that the small outfit sagged on her but it was better than the white hospital issued onesies that she had worn constantly. "I'll leave you alone with her." The nurse left the pair alone as Eve rocked the small baby back and forth. She searched the infant's face for features that were like her own but she couldn't find one. It was as if she hadn't even given birth to the child. From the top of her little head to the bottom of her feet she saw nothing but Tron. "It's okay baby. He'll figure out one day that he missed out on something special with you." She kissed the small cheek. Where she used to feel warmth was now turning colder and heavier by the second. Her baby was gone, she knew that now. The time passed and, although it had felt like only minutes to Eve as she rocked the baby back and forth, several hours went by before the nurses came to intervene. "It's time now, Eve. We need to take her now," they said. Taking her meant putting her in the morgue. They tried not to say those words but Eve knew what they meant. "But I don't want her to go....I can't believe she's gone." "Do you know what arrangements you will make yet?" asked a nurse, kindly. With so little money, her only option was cremation. That was another thing that pained her soul, to have her little princess burned and ground to dust because her father didn't care enough to send money for a proper burial. "I'll have her cremated and from there...I'm not sure," she admitted as she placed her baby girl down in the plastic crib. She said her goodbyes, giving her a kiss on the cheek. The nurse gave her a hug, a long embrace after spending six weeks together talking, crying, and laughing. Caring for Neveah had created a small bond between the two women. They let go of each other and without a word Eve left, trying to leave the hospital without breaking down on the way to her car. She took off her scrubs in a daze, throwing it all away in trash cans as she left. There was no one waiting to take her home like in the movies.

There was no long line of people coming with her to talk out her situation. Instead she walked to her car alone, thinking of all the things she had done wrong in her pregnancy. Partying into her eighth week when she realized she hadn't seen her period. A haphazard home pregnancy test that she stole from the dollar store gave her two blue lines instead of one. A clue that she was pregnant, but how could she have a baby? Eve was barely twenty-one, with no money, living in a studio apartment, struggling to pay rent. But sure enough, a trip to the clinic confirmed that she was one hundred percent with child. Telling Tron was okay at first. He seemed excited, taking her to dinner and going away for a nice weekend. But the next week she couldn't reach him and when she did, he said one sentence that crushed her soul. "I think you should get an abortion." The A word hadn't even crossed Eve's mind until he said it. When she refused he went into a rage, telling her that he would never be there and she would raise the baby on her own. "How am I supposed to tell my gal about this?" she heard him mutter when he thought she wasn't listening. She was so busy crying that she never told him that she heard those words, she never had a chance to make him apologize. He hung up that day and refused to take her calls. Tracking him down at work was the only way to put a stop to her endless worry. But when she finally saw him the unthinkable happened. She went into early labor brought on by the undue stress. Now she was getting into her cold car, her hands still smelling of the hospital antiseptic and almost numb as she tried to start her car. Everything was numb from her brain down to her feet so she barely could feel the gas pedal as she drove out of the parking lot. As she drove, she kept taking a long sniff of her hands, bathing her senses in the smell that reminded her of her firstborn. That smell would forever sit in her memory, linking her to a daughter that would never come home. That thought was stuck in her brain and now, in the comfort of her car, the thoughts finally became too much. She cried, the tears coming down as she held her stomach, where her baby should still have been. She wasn't due for another two months - a lot of time for a baby to grow and mature to be ready for the world. "I'm sorry I robbed you of that...I'm sorry that I was thinking about him and not about you," she sobbed, barely able to get the words out through her tears. From the hospital parking lot all the way to her house she cried and cried, endless tears that seemed to get worse and worse. Inside she checked into what was more like a jail than a studio apartment. All around were the reminders that she was supposed to be a mother. A crib sat in the corner and various baby clothes were there as well. Lying in bed she cried and cried with no one to console her and tell her it would be alright. She cried until she got sick. She cried herself to sleep and when she woke up she cried some more. Alone in her apartment with the shades drawn, she tried to find herself or at least figure out where she made the wrong turn. Every time she tried to track the problem she always ended up back in the same place. "Tron...it's all your fucking fault." She stared at the picture of them both that sat on her nightstand. The picture from one of their dates, basking in each other's company and seeming so deep in love. Little did she know it was all a show, a lie, and she was the side chick being used by a classic manipulator. "You lied to me... you told me that you loved me and you cared about me then...then you deserted me," she told the picture but it was stuck in time. Stuck back in the time when she knew nothing about the real Trontavious. "But you lied to not just me...you lied to us." She threw the picture and it landed perfectly in the middle of the dozen or so mementos scattered across her bed. Photos, documents, reports, and a DNA test request lay across her bed painting a picture of the man she had called her lover - Mr. Trontavious Carter. "I hate you...I fucking hate you!!" she screamed at his photographed face, but that didn't do her anger justice. She had vowed not to do this but after being ignored she had no choice. She leaped up to her feet and went in search of her phone. With the sun just now setting, Eve grabbed her phone and dialed the number she had memorized. "Hello, Auto Sales, this is Jessica..." "Yes I need to speak with Trontavious Carter, please." The phone went silent, no clicks, rings, or a request to hold on. Instead there was nothing but awkward silence on the line. "Hello?" Eve looked at the receiver making sure the call hadn't dropped. "Hello…" "Yes…yes ma'am," the receptionist's responded, her move to unmute the line was way more obvious than she tried to make it and pushing Eve further to the end of irritation. "May I ask who's calling?" "Why?" Eve snapped back at her, more annoyed by the second. "Can't you just put me through?" Why does it matter who it is? "Umm…I'm sorry ma'am," the receptionist said robotically, like she was reading from a script. "Trontavious no longer works here." The wheels in Eve's head started turning. He told her to say this. He is avoiding me, she told herself as her anger began to rise. "What do you mean? He was working there a month ago…now all of a sudden poof…he's gone?" She looked at the phone as if she were being tricked in some way. "Put Tron on the phone, bitch," he growled into the receiver, wishing she could jump through the phone and strangle the receptionist with her bare hands. "Excuse me ma'am…Don't curse at me." Thoughts of her lost child tumbled around in her head and in an instant Eve's temper exploded through her mouth and into the phone. "PUT TRON ON THE PHONE, BITCH!" she screamed but before she was done pronouncing the last syllable the phone went dead. "FUCK!" Throwing the phone on the bed she balled her fist up and sent it through the wall. Plaster and drywall dust covered her arm as she screamed, wishing that the hole was in Tron's head instead of in her bedroom wall. "He's there. He just doesn't want to talk to you," she reasoned with herself, but that line of reasoning was unacceptable. "No...no... no… that's still not a reason," she told herself back. She needed him to understand that this wasn't right. "Regardless of that, he still missed her birth. He missed everything. Now she's gone and he never even knew her name!" She began to cry, seeing flashes of the life she had planned go up in smoke then reappear as her dead daughter dressed in pink. The shaking and crying made her knees buckle as she sobbed, crying out for help. Eventually the tears dried and the choking stopped and Eve was left holding her legs and rocking back and forth with a focused gaze on the nightstand picture. After a while the picture became real to her. He wasn't in an inanimate frame but was an actual person held in time inside her bedroom. With the same smile and expression, he stood in front of her with a cheesy grin. "After all you've put me through. You're just going to smile?" she asked the hologram Tron that was now growing bigger in her space. "You know what Tron… I'm going to make you wish that you never met me. That you had never been born. And I'm going to make you regret missing my child's life. With everything in me I will make you suffer you sonofabitch!" Eve yelled, jumping to her feet. In her reality she was grabbing Tron by the throat, squeezing it until the smile faded away but what she was really holding was the broken picture frame with broken glass cutting through her hand. A crunched picture of Tron was in the middle of the mess, covered in Eve's own blood as the glass ripped through her soft skin. She wanted to scream from the pain, from the sight of her own flesh being torn apart by Tron but the screams wouldn't leave her mouth. In fact, her lips wouldn't even part. Instead she walked calmly to the bathroom. Grabbing peroxide, bandages, and tweezers she removed the bits of glass with the precision of a surgeon, one by one without making a sound. The picture of Tron was now scratched and stained with blood and Eve had no intention of changing that. She didn't even bother to wash off the blood. "That's how your ass deserves to be. Covered in blood you bitch…" She coughed and spit a perfect glob of her saliva onto the picture. Looking in the mirror, the bags under her eyes, messy bun, and scraggly eyebrows meant nothing. She had a calling now, something she had to do. It was clear in her spirit that Tron needed to be taught a lesson. He had to pay, and the best way to do that was to pour every bit of energy she had into his demise.

Chapter Eighteen

DONESHA

After several needle sticks and spreading my legs for a tissue sample I was now waiting. They said they would have some results today so I tried to stay calm and not read the scary disease information covering the exam room walls. All this information on everything from Syphilis to HPV was littered everywhere giving me a million ideas of what could be going on. Please God don't let me have a disease. Anything but that, I prayed as I waited. I tried shifting my mind to other things, like my wedding. I wanted royal purple and gold as our colors but Tron wanted red and white. I wanted to get married within the next year but he wanted to wait a few years. Things weren't matching up and I guess I had no way to tell him he was wrong. Here I was in a clinic getting a checkup because of another man. A man that was my mother's husband. The shit sounded sick when you said it all together. Every thought I had was from one extreme of fucked up to the next. "Alright…" The doctor swooped in with a few papers in her hand. She smoother her jet black hair in its ponytail and pushed her gold wire-rimmed glasses back onto the bridge of her nose. "We have to wait about a week to get the pap results back and around the same time for the blood work," she said with her Russian accent so thick I could barely understand her. "That's fine…but what about..?" I pointed to the papers. "Is there anything in there about the Trick that I asked you about?" "Yes. You are positive for trichomonas." "WHAT?!" I screamed, as if she had given me the disease. "Not to worry, we just have to give you a prescription and you will be good as new. In your condition just taking the pill form will be fine to clear things up." My condition? The doctor acted like this was nothing. I prided myself on being disease free and now I had something. Fucking Clarence. I'm going to fuck him up. I felt like running out of the office and beating his ass right now. How am I going to tell Tron he needs to get treated? "I feel sick...I think I'm going to be sick." A nurse knocked on the door seconds later. A tray of medicine and a needle confirmed that they were very serious about what she had told me. "Wait a second. We have to make sure that won't interfere with the other situation," the doctor cautioned. My ears perked up when I heard that. "Is that all? Is it something else?" Did I have herpes or something? "Oh you're right... just pills for her." The nurse said putting the needle back on the tray with a smile. What the hell is she smiling about? "What is going on?" Somebody better tell me something or I was going to flip out really quick. "We tested your urine and it came back positive for HcG. The pregnancy hormone." Now she was just messing with me. I had to laugh at that. "No ma'am. You see, I knew you had the wrong results." I shooed her away, laughing at the audacity of this lady. "You have to do better than this doc. You can't go around giving out false results."

This is what I got for coming to the free clinic, but I had waited long enough, three whole weeks since I heard my Mama say that Clarence had a disease. I had fucked him since then without a condom, further proving how stupid I was. Now I was here to take care of my health and they feed me this bullshit. "Why do you say that? These came from your tests." This so-called doctor didn't know me or my history and if she did she wouldn't have come to me with these lies about a pregnancy test. I probably would have believed her. "Ma'am...I was molested when I was a child. I was told that I would never have kids so please. Go get my real results." These damn clinic doctors never seemed to care. They were so careless, even giving me the wrong damn test results. She paused and cleaned her glasses with her white physician's coat but that still wasn't enough to get her to see my side. "When was your last period?" I shrugged, she was still reaching for something to prove this lie. "I don't know whatever I wrote on the paper. I'm damn near in med school so I don't have time to keep up with my period anymore," I laughed, just being happy to have on matching clothes and shoes. "Okay, I'll be right back." She and the nurse left just as quickly as they came and I started to walk out right behind her. But I waited. I wanted to see the look on her face when she figured it out and that she was going to have to apologize. A few moments later, the door cracked a bit then shoved open by doctor, now pushing a cart. I saw a monitor and something in my brain finally registered that this was an ultrasound machine. "We double checked and these are your results Ms. Hill. And we will do an ultrasound to confirm that." I didn't have time to think. They were already plugging up the machine and slathering my stomach with a cool gel. "I told you...I'm not pregnant this is just…" But then I saw it. I watched the screen and a little cell stuck out like a sore thumb. "Yep, there you have it. You are pregnant." She rolled the ultrasound wand around a bit to get a better angle. This morning when I left the house I wasn't expecting any of this and now I was in tears watching a small monitor with my baby on it. "This isn't real...there is no way," I whispered. "Do you want me to print one for you?" she asked. "No...I want you to tell me how is this possible." "Are you okay Ms. Hill. Do you need water?" the nurse asked but I didn't need shit but the truth. "I was molested when I was younger. The doctors...they have always said that...I could never..." I thought back to that time and instantly the tears came sprouting out of my eyes. This was a part of my life that I had tried to bury but still I remembered vividly the number of tears I cried after hearing I would never have kids. As a child you can't fully wrap your mind around the concept but as I got older my hate and anger towards that day and time brought more and more understanding. I was barren, excruciating periods were all I had left and because of that I wished every day that my grandmother could come alive and die again. It was all her fault that this happened and now her spirit was toying with me. "Do you know why the doctors said that specifically?" the doctor interrupted my thoughts. "Something about scaring and trauma. I'm not exactly sure but I know they said it wasn't possible." She hit a button on the machine and a small printer began to buzz. "Are you sure you're okay Ms. Hill? You are shaking."

Looking down at my hands, they were trembling but this was equivalent to being told you are going to die and someone comes back and says that you were fine the whole time. "Well, whatever was wrong has now been corrected." She passed the small ultrasound picture to me. "You are going to be a mother." Holding the picture I felt joy for a fleeting instant before a problem came into my thoughts. "Do you know how far along I am?" My mind raced like a rapid fire rolodex trying to figure out what dates I fucked who on. Some days I overlapped. I would see Tron in the morning and Clarence that night. It was a crazy time of ho activities that I wouldn't have admitted to my closest friend. I wasn't proud of it but now there was a child, a child that could belong to my fiancé or to my mother's husband. The thought alone made my head hurt. "Looks to be about eight weeks from calculations." Eight weeks, I needed a calendar. I needed to know what happened eight weeks ago and who I was with. "Congratulations." Everything else she said was just like a mumble. I tried to pay attention but none of it mattered anymore. I prided myself on being clean, never having a disease and now I was just like all those women I talked about. How could I have been caught slipping? It had to be Clarence, there was no way that Tron was messing around. That made things even worse. Out of the clinic I walked like a mechanical robot to my car and sat there in a daze. There was a new life inside me and as sat there, I didn't know where to go first. Who knew if Tron was the daddy or if it was Clarence? I was diseased, pregnant, and confused about who got me this way. And that worst part was that I didn't know how to get out. I was all set to drive home and drown myself in the bathtub when my phone rang. "Hello?" I answered. "Yes...is this...Donesha?" I didn't recognize the voice and no number showed on the screen. "This is she." As soon as I said that, the woman started laughing. "What can I do for you?" This felt weird and with all the things that were now swirling in my head I didn't have the time or the patience for anybody's bullshit. "You can't...not yet. But you will soon." Then the phone went dead....

Chapter Nineteen
TRON

I've cheated on Donesha more times than I could count and it always went the same way. I got my dick wet then I came home, took a shower, and I was back to myself. But not after Yvette. I couldn't stop thinking about her, she had turned me into some tender, dick ass little boy after just one time. I don't know what it was, maybe how she challenged me, slapping me across my face. IT made me mad enough to hit her but instead I gave her a dick lashing. I've never been a tender dick about a bitch but somehow she stayed on my mind. I don't know if it was the sex or maybe it was the money she told me about. Either way, I tried my best over the last few weeks to stay away. After that first time, I told myself I would never do that again. I got good at avoiding her, spent Christmas with my side of the family and planned on telling Donesha that I wanted to stay at home by ourselves this New Year's Eve. But somebody else had other plans. It was like she read my mind when she sent me a text to meet up and talk. The message was simple, meet her on the edge of town to talk. A talk turned into an agreement and on that cold chilly morning the agreement lead me to this hotel. It had outdoor hallways and wall unit air conditioner but it had a bed and a bed was all we needed. Now I was breaking her back on New Year's Eve. "Fuck me...Fuck me Tron..." Her voice bounced off the cheap motel walls. Our clothes were scattered around the room as I bent her ass over grudge fuck style. I was giving her my signature move where I grab a fist full of a bitch's hair and hold on tight as I grind into her ass from behind. The pope...Jesus...even my own damn mother could have told me that I was going to be fucking my girl's mom and I would have laughed at they ass but the proof was in the pudding, or the pussy rather.

Because I was dick deep in Yvette as she called my name. "Tron...oh Tron..yes...Like that baby...right there." Chicks went wild when I put in my signature move of ass grinding and pelvis pumping but none of them went wilder than Yvette. She screamed and hollered, making me feel like I had the biggest dick in the world. Usually I had to do all the work but with Yvette, we moved as one. "Shit girl..." She pushed her ass back into me. Her pussy so wet and soft that my dick was swimming in a marshmallow. I held on as she took control popping her pussy back on me as she led my free hand around the front of her to play with her clit. "Yes...yes...just like that." She encouraged me as we kept moving together in our own little grind bounce dance. The room spun and my heart pounded like a snare drum. I felt the cum rise up and within seconds I was exploding inside of her. "Yes daddy...come inside me." I felt like a king as she pushed her pussy back on me while I filled her with my seeds. "Oh shit..." I pulled out as I came out of the trance. "I came in you. I'm tripping...fuck fuck fuck..." We had done that at least twice, popping through all of our condoms when we decided that skin to skin was the best way, like the first time we met. Now all these weeks later I couldn't keep my hands off her. "Don't worry. I'm taking birth control still. It's okay." She smiled, so sure, as she panted out of breath. "I like it when you cum in me anyway. When Clarence tries to go down on me I imagine he's sucking your nut out of my pussy." "Damn girl...I don't want to imagine that." It was like a bull had head butted me in the stomach. "I'm just saying I don't respect his ass. You're a real man...I just wish..." She looked away, not wanting to say it. Neither of us talked much about the whole arrangement. We just moved like two secret lovers, booking motels on the edge of town or sneaking in text messages on apps that held no names. It happened so quickly it was hard for me to even digest it. One minute we were just son-and mother-in-law, now we were...fucking. "How long...?" I tried to find the words but we had to talk about this. "How long do you think we are going to do this?" She shrugged at that. Patting a towel between her legs she just kept fanning herself like she didn't have a care in the world. "Do you even care if we get caught?" I asked. "You see...I'll answer your question like this. People all around the world are doing fucked up shit. This one thing that I'm doing here isn't going to change the course of history." She was extremely cynical when she wanted to be but sweet at other times. "But Clarence and Donesha..." "Fuck them...We keep doing what we're doing but don't mention them to me okay," She snapped and I thought she was going to bite my damn head off. It was an honest question for someone having an affair, but to Yvette whatever I said was fighting words. "Look I'm just under a lot of stress with lawyers and..." She started talking about court dates but I had no clue what she was talking about. "Are you in some kind of trouble or something?" I began to sit up looking around as if the FBI had the room tapped. I always wondered how her husband made his money. Sometimes I joked with Donnie that his ass was going to get locked up one day. She hated when I said that shit. "No..." Yvette laughed. "I guess it's not funny though. But my Moms will. There was...well..." She looked away. "What...did she leave you a house in Europe or some shit?" I had to make her laugh. The situation with granny dying was crazy. One day she was walking around cursing people and the next she was in a coma. "No, she left me and the girls about six hundred thousand dollars." I almost fell off the bed when she said it. "What? Are you fucking serious." "Chill…" She shook her head as she put her bra on. "What do you mean chill? That's a lot of fucking money." "I know, that's why I'm not in a rush to give it to the girls. I know they might blow right through it." I thought about Donesha and her crazy ass spending habits. She could make a hundred dollars disappear in ten seconds. "So what are you going to do?" "Well, I have a prenup with Clarence. I just have to stick with his ass for five years and I get everything. So I'm going to save my inheritance money and try to push this out as long as possible so it's not included in the divorce." "What?" "Yeah I don't want it included." "But what about Nene And Lonnie?" "What about them? They're fine." "But they need money. Hell, Nene is going to be in med school. I'm supposed to make a five thousand dollar payment in a few months." Since I lost my job I had no clue where that payment was coming from. "She does…I don't give a damn about what she needs to pay for." She stormed off going into the bathroom slamming the door. "Yvette…don't be like that." The faucet turned on and she locked me out, leaving me with my dick swinging in the hotel. Six hundred thousand dollars divided by three people was a lot of dough. It was enough to put a down payment on my own dealership and get a lot of shit taken care of. She came out of the bathroom with her lip poking out. "What's wrong?" "You're judging me. I didn't know I was going to fall in love with you and…" "What's that on you?" I turned her around looking at her back and saw a bruise I didn't notice before. "Oh… that's nothing." She quickly tried to cover it up but it was too late. "Nothing? It's red and black. Did you hit something?" She froze like a deer in headlights as I examined her. "Were you in a car accident?" She moved away from me as I touched it, wincing in pain. "Did Clarence…" "Just leave it alone." "Are you fucking serious?" I shouldn't have cared but for some reason thinking of him putting his hands on her made my face hot. "Just leave it be. I'm going to leave him soon enough." "But what if he beats the hell out of you in the meantime?" I had questions and it seemed she just wanted to leave it alone. "Trust me he isn't going to do that. I just want to enjoy our time, I already have a plan to get them back." "Them?" "Him and the bitch he's fucking with. Don't worry about it. The shit is a long drawn out story that I don't want to talk about right now. She had more secrets than a damn diary. Watch out playa. These chicks gone get you fucked up. I heard Ro in my head and now sitting in the position I was in, I could believe him. I hadn't talked to him since I got fired. He would be really surprised to hear about the shit that I was into now. You know what...I'm going to take a shower real quick." I watched her now and I could see where Donesha got her ass from. What the fuck are you doing? I felt like I was floating in a cloud. Losing my job and her getting me drunk life just seemed to spiral and before I knew it we were fucking. What was I supposed to do? I played a game over the last few weeks. What would happen if Donesha found out? I went from a few different extremes. In one, Donesha would stab me in my sleep; the other was of her crying, crushing her life and heart into a million pieces. You could have left...my mother...MY FUCKING MOTHER. I would try to console her but what could I say. "Baby I was over your mom's house and she was massaging me and somehow my dick came out." She would kill me, no way she wouldn't. As if she felt me talking about her, my phone rang filling up the hotel room. "Didn't I tell you no cell phones?" She was in the shower but somehow she heard my phone as soon as it started ringing. "Tron turn it off." "Chill, "s you're daughter." The bathroom door slammed like she was some fucking teenager. It was like the bitch was trying to run me. "Hello..." I heard nothing but crying, the muffled tears of Donesha. She knew, she had to know. I sat up in the bed waiting to hear her screams. "Donesha... what is it? Talk to me baby." "I need to see you...I need to see you right now." "What's wrong?" "Right now Tron. Get home please, I can't talk to you about this over the phone." "Okay...I'm on my way." Hanging up, I got dressed like I was going to my funeral. Coming out of the bathroom, Yvette instantly started going off. "Where the hell are you going? I told you no cell phones. I can't believe this shit…" She took the wooden hangers from the hotel closet and started tossing them at me like basketballs. "Yo what the fuck is wrong with you!" "I can't believe you…" She cried like I was the one that beat her. She acted like I raped her. I watched and took cover. "Yo chill the fuck out Yvette…what is wrong with you?" "Just leave…this was a fucking mistake. Just leave." She ran back into the bathroom slamming the door like I was chasing her. "Just leave. I can't believe I did this shit." I wanted to go after her, see what the hell her problem was but between my phone ringing and the sound of glass breaking in the bathroom I put my clothes on and raced out of there. You've fucked up this time Tron." Ro was in my head again. It was like everybody was in my damn head except me. My phone rang again, trying to make it down to the lobby had my snapping as I answered. "WHAT?!" Instead of tears, crying, or yelling I heard laughter. "Who the fuck is this?" "I know you better take some of that bass out ya voice nigga." The crackling of his voice let me know who it was instantly.

"Yo Melo...Wassup man. My bad I thought..." "Have you thought about my money?" "Umm. I haven't forgot dawg I..." I tried to explain as I waited for the elevator but he wouldn't let me. At every explanation he stopped me. Changed my words around on me. "You shouldn't forget owing a nigga twenty fucking thousand dollars." "Yeah dawg. I know but..." "But what nigga? I should have had a payment a week ago." I stopped talking and started listening. "What, you ain't got shit to say?" "Naw man... I don't for real." "Well word on the street says you got fired from your job. You fucking up double time. I had some cars I had planned for over there." That was the other half of my dilemma. Me losing my job fucked a few ventures I had going on. Not just my money but side hustles that ran through the dealership. "FUCK..." everything was falling down on me at one time. I needed a lot of money and real fucking fast. I had only one way to get it and back in that hotel room was the pussy that held all the money. Fuck her out of it. Shit goes south at least you got the money. With slow steps I walked back, turning my cell phone off. Back in the room she was out of the bathroom now sitting on the bed naked, her makeup running. "Why are you back?" She looked delicate like a flower and I was a honey bee coming to sting her ass. "I just wanted to see if you were okay...I wanted to make sure that there was nothing bad between us..." I eased back into the room choosing my words carefully like a pastor in a full church. "I'm just sorry...I'm sorry if you're hurt and that this happened." "I give...I give everything to everyone else and I get stepped on. By my husband...by my fucking kids. My mother is gone and...I'm just alone. No one gives a damn." I went to her, wrapping my arms around her as she cried digging her nails into my back as she cried. "I'm sorry...I'm so sorry." I felt the heat from her body. The volcano of her heart exploding and here I was trying not to get burned. A phone rang but it wasn't mine. Instead hers vibrated on the bed and she went to it instantly, shielding herself with a sheet. "Yes...yes...Yes I can do that. Okay... Yes. I'm the executor of the estate. Right...okay." In seconds she was off and a smile stretched across her face. "You okay...?" "I'm more than okay." She said smiling. "The insurance money…We got more than I thought." "Really… How much?" "Three…three hundred thousand." I damn near fell to my knees. "Shit…" "They want to settle everything now…" "So what are you going to do?" "I don't know. I still don't want to tell the girls yet. I want to get things set up for them first." I started counting. As she said it. Something just occurred to me. I had something going with all three of them. What if… "Nine hundred thousand dollars…Split three ways." She started crying again but this looked like tears of joy. "If Mama didn't do shit, she did one thing right." I had the thought but how the fuck could I pull it off. If I could get fifty thousand from all three of them and keep the shit quiet it would change everything. I could pay off Rollie and…" "TRON!" "Huh…yeah…" "Did you hear me…?" "Naw I'm sorry I was…" "What should I do? Should I tell the girls or keep this to myself?" I didn't have a plan yet. I needed a plan and I needed to talk to Lanesha first. "Just hold on to this. Hold off for a minute. What about your husband?" "Fuck him…I'm yours now." She said kissing me deeply in my mouth, like we were getting married.

"Ain't that right?" How could I tell her no? If I did, my whole world would blow up more than it was now. I had to have something to hang on to. "Yeah you're right baby. It's you and me." I lied like I did to all females, but she wanted more. "So you're going to leave her. When I leave Clarence of course." She put me on the spot like I was sitting on trial. Her eyes on me, nowhere to run or hide. I had to secure one of them. Out of the three, Yvette was the most important. She controlled all of the bags while Lanesha and Donesha took what was given to them. I was flying above myself again looking down on the disaster. Not only did I kiss her but I pulled away the sheet. Pushing her back on the bed I traced my hands down over her body as I went to my knees. Eye level with her snatch I pulled her to the edge of the bed. With a smile I pushed my head face first into her juicy center as she clawed at the bed. It wasn't right, I was dead ass wrong, but I needed this and there was already no turning back. I was all into this shit. Now I just had to make this bitch cum to secure my future then make it home to Donnie.

Chapter Twenty

LANESHA

I raced to the house getting there just as Tron was pulling in behind me. I hadn't seen him since the day I bailed him out of jail. He still hasn't gave me my money back, but I wasn't here to talk about that today, I needed to find out what was going on with my sister, but seeing him frantic made the alarms pop off in my head. She knows. "Hey?" he said as I got out of the car. He had a shit look on his face like he was guilty of something. "What's going on?" "Happy new year to you too…" I rolled my eyes at that. He still looked good in his suit and I could smell his intoxicating cologne from where I stood a few feet away. But that was as close as I wanted to get to the man. I told myself if he didn't come around before the clock struck midnight on the new year then we would be done. And here we were a week into the new year and I hadn't heard a word from him. "What's going on? Why am I here?" I asked him, avoiding the lame flirting that he liked to do. "I don't know...she called and told me to come home, that it was something she needed to talk to me about." "She said the same thing to me. You don't think that she knows about...you know?" He looked around for a second up to the house and shrugged his shoulders. "Only one way to find out." We both walked to the door. Me behind him because if we walked into an ambush I was going to let his ass get hit first. But instead going into the house there was light jazz playing, incense lit, and my sister on the couch with a smile from ear to ear. "Baby what's going on?" He went to her, hugging her like I wasn't even in the room. Relax he isn't you're man, I had to tell myself so I could stay calm but a big part of me wanted to slap him in the face for disrespecting me over and over again. I'm cool enough to fuck, bail him out of jail, and be his on call concubine but I'm not good enough to be his companion. Seeing them hugged up made me want to throw up but I swallowed my pride and gave my sister a hug. "What's up Sis are you okay?" Our relationship was rocky since the Thanksgiving night reveal of her relationship with Clarence, if that's what you would call it. She hadn't clarified exactly what they were to me. And since I figured out that Tron wasn't worth fighting for I stopped caring. Now I was in her living room sitting down on her loveseat pretending that I don't want to jump in her man's arms and kiss him all over. "I just wanted my favorite people around me." She smiled a little devilish grin. "That's it baby?...you had me rush home." he tickled her and she squealed like a toddler as they played. I cleared my throat letting the love birds know I was still in the room and had no intention of watching them make out. "Okay, well sis I love you. I'm gonna head out." I turned to leave seeing that whatever she wanted must have been some type of false alarm. "Hold on..." She laughed. "Why are you leaving so soon? I cooked for you." "Oh yeah, baby, you cooked?" Tron asked taking off his suit jacket, a nice fresh hickey on his neck. I glared at it. "What? So now you want us to eat." This was making no sense, she was making no sense and seeing Tron all over her and affectionate was making my ass itch. "Yep, go get the food out the oven. Baby go help her." She pushed Tron towards the kitchen with me. I felt this was a setup but we smiled and walked slowly into the kitchen anyway. "It's in the oven." Tron at my side walking slow right along with me. "Is it a bomb?" he whispered laughing. Everything was a joke to him, but I ignored his dumb ass and pulled open the oven. "Ohh shit." A set of rolls with an ultrasound sat on the top rack. "BABY!!!!" he screamed, running back in the living room. "We're having a baby!" I could hear them laughing, Tron screaming, but in my heart I was crying. Fix your face, be happy. Taking the ultrasound back in the living room. the first thing I saw was Tron's smile. The expression across his face was joy like I've never seen, even when we were together in our most intimate moments. "Congratulations!" I pretended to be excited. Screaming and jumping up and down even squeezing out a few fake tears. "How do you feel?" "I feel good. A little tired. I don't think I'm going to Mom's party tonight. Don't feel like talking to her. Don't know if she's going to be happy or tell me that I'm screwing up by not being done with school." "Well...I gotta go because she wants me to pick up some things," I lied. I had to go before I cried in her face and slapped the dreads off Tron's head. "But I love you. Can't wait to see my little niece or nephew." I rubbed her stomach as if something could be felt already. "Alright sis...Love you," she said squeezing me tight. I wanted to ask her if was she sure the baby was Tron's, but who knew at this point. I was done trying to connect the dots and as Tron sat beside her on the couch, he couldn't even look me in the eye. "Is it okay if I tell Mom or do you want to tell her?" She thought about it for a moment. "You can tell her." "Alright...love you. Boy, this is a happy new year's gift for real." I backed towards the door waving and smiling but once I made it out into the cold, I ran to my car. I jumped inside and burned rubber, right as the tears began to fall. "You're so stupid...stupid...stupid... stupid," I told myself, banging on the steering wheel. But yet again I was the one on the outside looking in. My plans to expose her and take Tron were ruined. Now I had no man, no baby. Happy fucking New Year to me. I got to my mother's house and immediately started drinking - shot after shot until I no longer felt the pain. As the guests started pouring in, I was finally able to peel myself off the sofa and tell my mother the news. I waited until she was in the kitchen by herself to spill the beans. "Ma…" "What's wrong with you? I saw you over there sitting all sunken in the couch. You lose your man or something?" She laughed but the comment cut me like a knife. "Donnie is pregnant." I watched and saw the color drain from her face. "She's what?" "Pregnant…" "Where is she?" "She's at home. They said they weren't coming." "They?" "Her and Tron. I went over there…she told us both at the same time." Ma looked weak, finding a seat at the kitchen table and rubbing her temples like she was getting a massive migraine. "Hey Lanesha. I wanted you to meet Bryan." Clarence came around the corner looking like the snake that he was. Since the day I caught him with my sister, he hadn't said two words to me until today. Before I could say hi to his cute friend, my mother butted in. "Donesha is pregnant." I had to laugh, Clarence looked like he'd seen a ghost. He fumbled over his words trying to get his thoughts together. "Ummm...wow...ummm..." "FIVE MINUTES UNTIL THE NEW YEAR!" someone yelled as Clarence stumbled over his words. I was tired of holding secrets and being the one getting shitted on. "Wow, that's awesome. I guess were going to be grandparents." Clarence cracked a fake smile and I had enough. "You want a drink?" Bryan asked as I stepped away. "No...I want to get out of here..." I told him honestly, walking away. As I made my way back to the living room I heard keys jingle. "My car is outside. I'm sober...where do you want to go?" He was fine, a short faded cut and deep brown skin with sparking white teeth that shone at me. His cologne was intoxicating and right now I wanted to be anywhere but here. "Wherever... you lead the way," I told him and he took my hand leading me out of the party into the cold. His car was nice, leather seats that warmed up seconds after he started the engine. "Is this a Benz?" "Yep." he said revving the engine. "And your name is Bryan?" "Yeah...a friend of Clarence." I normally wouldn't have trusted anyone that knew Clarence, but I had a good feeling about this guy. "So where are we going?" He smiled when I asked that. "Just trust me...we're going to make this night magical." I did as he said, sitting back as he turned on the radio and sped out of my mother's subdivision. I wanted the new year to mean a new life for me. No more Tron, no more Donesha, and no more settling. This year it would be all about me.

Chapter Twenty One
CLARENCE

It was the new year but I wasn't shit happy about it. I had to act like I was happy that Donesha was pregnant but on the inside I was beyond mad. But I kept it cool, especially when I saw Bryan leaving with Lonnie. At least a part of my plan was going right. Waking up New Year's Day, my wife did what she did best, and that was hit the sales. She was up and out of the house before noon and that gave me my opportunity to investigate the truth. I had to hear it from Donesha's mouth, look her in the eye and see what was really happening. I waited outside their house for Tron to leave. If I knew nothing else, he was a workaholic and getting to the dealership on New Year's Day was prime buying time. Sure enough, within an hour I saw his car backing out of the garage. I waited until he was gone off the block before I went up to the door. Knocking and ringing the bell she opened up like she was surprised to see me. "Hey...what are you doing here?" She looked around on the street. "He's gone, I saw him leave. I need to talk to you." I didn't wait to be invited in, just strolled right past her. "Clarence you can't be doing this. You can't just pop up..." "Is it true?" "Is what true?" "Don't play dumb. Are you pregnant?" She looked down and whispered so low I could barely hear her. "What?" "I said yes," she said, finally picking her head back up. "Is it mine?" Donesha had no answer to that. "It's a simple question yes or no." "I don't know okay...just leave me alone." "You need to get an abortion." "A what? Clarence get the fuck out of my house. I'm not aborting my baby." "But what if it's mine...what will that do with me and your mom and the money..." "What money?" she demanded. I had said too much. I tried to back track but it was too late. "What are you talking about Clarence. What money?" I couldn't tell her about the inheritance. The shit wasn't final yet or something that Yvette told me. It hadn't even been a year yet and I knew these things took time. "Don't change the subject. You can't do this messy shit, you hear me." I took a step towards her. "Now get rid of it. I'll give you the money." She looked at me like I had six eyes. "I want you out of my house...now!" "Bitch I'm not going nowhere. You know that's probably my baby." I was ready to hit her, make her have a miscarriage if she wasn't willing to do what the fuck I was telling her. It was a lot of money on the line and I wasn't losing it over her ass. "Bitch? Who you calling a bitch?" She backed away as I kept walking towards her. "What if I told my mama about what the fuck we've been doing." I took another step closer, looking her dead in her eyes. "You tell your Mama and I'm gonna kill you and that baby." The terror in her eyes was familiar. She looked just like Yvette right now. "Yeah your Mama looks at me the same way when I beat her ass. You wanna be next?" "What? Get the fuck out!" She ran towards the kitchen and I heard a drawer open but I didn't give a fuck about her grabbing a knife. "Come here bitch…" As I made my way to the kitchen, I heard the garage. "That's Tron. He just went out to the store, now he's back. You better get out of here before I have him fuck you up." "This ain't over." I wanted to stay, fight him and kill her but that would have to be done another day. Instead I ran out the patio door. In the back yard I walked around to the side and jumped the fence heading to my car like nothing happened. I had too much money on the line and too many bills to pay to be fucking with this young broad. Should have kept your dick in your pants. That was always my problem but I had to secure my future. These bitches weren't going to worry me. I had to deal with this issue and if she wasn't going to listen to me, then I had to get someone that would make her listen. Driving away I took out my phone and called the one person that could persuade anybody. My brother Bryan.

Chapter Twenty Two

BRYAN

Bryan jerked awake, sitting straight up in the bed. He tried to readjust his sight for a moment, not knowing whether he was in a gun fight or a shallow grave. All of those things were possibilities in his line of work but everything made sense when he saw her. Sleeping peacefully beside him was Lanesha, her face relaxed and serene as she slept naked, wrapped in his legs with a sheet haphazardly strewn across her body. His phone buzzed on the nightstand, calling for his attention. Slipping out of bed like a stealth ninja, Bryan made his way to the bathroom to take the call. "Hello…"

"What happened?" Clarence asked sounding frantic.

"What do you mean?" "Did you see if she knew anything?" "These things take time. I can't find all of that out in one night." Clarence made a grunt of frustration from his end of the line. "I need this to not be a situation. I need you to find this out for me." If this were a regular client, Bryan would have hung up the phone but it was Clarence, someone Bryan considered to be family so he took a deep breath and tried to stay calm. "Listen, I'll let you know in a few days what's going on." "That's not good enough." Standing in his bathroom in briefs and a bare chest he wanted to be back in bed with the warm soft body, not arguing with this old man. "C...let me do my job man," he whispered. "I got this." "You better." Without another word, Clarence hung up leaving Bryan staring at the phone. He hated disrespect and killed people for far less offense. Breathe Bryan...breathe..." he told himself, rinsing his face with cold water. He left the bathroom and went back into his master suite. He watched Lanesha sleeping like a baby for a few moments, thinking about their night together, how it was the most fun that he had in years. They laughed, danced, and partied till the wee hours of the morning. Too tired to go home they decided to go back to his place where a love making session for the ages ensued. They came together as one as if they had been together for years. Lanesha had been so gentle, rubbing him and massaging his aching muscles. Kissing and caressing him and she wasn't afraid to go down on him first without being asked. He was surprised and excited about entering her like it was his first time being with a woman. Now he crept around the room looking for her purse. Finding it under a pile of discarded clothes he went through it as quietly as he could so as not to disturb Sleeping Beauty. Nothing in the purse was interesting until he went through her phone. Going through her text messages there was one person in particular that had been texting her all night long. Answer me. Hello So you're going to ignore me We need to talk Happy New Year I guess So you're really not going to answer !!!!!! And the texts went on and on from a person that was in her phone as nothing other than T. Who the fuck is T? He didn't know, but a bit of jealousy rose in his throat. What the fuck is wrong with me? Before he could answer she began to stir in the bed, sending him to put her purse back where he found it, along with her phone, and slip back into bed right as she peeked open her eyes. "Happy New Year," she said smiling with her eyes sparkling. "Happy New Year to you beautiful." He told her pulling her close. "I had a great time last night." It was the truth, this part of him wasn't a part of the job he was working on. She laughed wrapping her arms around him. "Me too. You know I don't usually get down like this," she told him. "I'm glad you did this time." Their lips touched and tongues wrestled til the chiming sound of her phone entered the air. "Ugh...I'm so tired of that damn phone." "Then leave it. You want to go get something to eat?" "Yeah, can I take a shower here first?" "Sure...go right ahead." Damn, a girl that wants to shower first. Bryan said to himself as he watched Lanesha's sultry stroll to the bathroom. "I won't be long." She winked at him retreating to the bathroom. As soon as he heard the shower running and the sound of her stepping inside, Bryan dove for her phone. Looking through it, it was the same number, the T person was texting again. I can't believe you won't answer me. But Bryan could believe it. He listened to her hum, a soft melody filling his space where silence and loneliness usually consumed him. It felt good to have someone else around, especially a female that was so easy going and cool to be around. I know this is a job but I like her, he reasoned with himself. Stuffing the phone back into her purse he made a decision. Waiting for his house guest to finally get out of the shower, she soon emerged in a towel with her body glistening and damp. "So, where can we go eat?" Bryan shrugged, he had only one question on his mind. "You...you don't have a boyfriend or anything do you?" Lanesha was totally honest. Taking a deep breath and smiling to keep from crying she gave him the truth. "I was with someone but it was complicated. Now I'm done with him," she reasoned and that was all that Bryan needed to hear. He was the king of complicated so he could understand. "And you're done for sure?" "Yes... why you got someone in mind for me?" She asked letting her towel fall to the floor. "I might have someone in mind," he said, rising from the bed and going to the

Nubian goddess in the doorway. He wanted to devour her, keep her all to himself, but for right now he would settle for bringing her into his bed. But Bryan knew he had found something special. Now he just had to figure out how to keep her from harm's way. Months Later

an hour. "Will your husband be in? He's not on the trust is he…?" Mr. Abitol asked and it sounded like a damn joke. Clarence wasn't going to know anything about this. I almost spit the water out onto the desk. "No sir…Just me." Mama would have never allowed that. She didn't trust a man further than she could throw them. She asked me once, did I have a savings account of my own? When I told her I didn't believe in having money separate from my husband she damn near cursed me out. "Little girl…turn off your damn heart and turn on your brain." Mama told me that so many times it was like I had it tattooed on me. It was her mantra, the mission statement of how we lived for so many years. Driving home I thought about my Mama. The way she turned her lip up when she was mad, how she could flip anything around, and how, over all of that, she was the sneakiest bitch I knew. "What do you think of me, Mama, huh?" I imagined she could see me and was shaking her head at all the sick moves I was making. "It's you…it's all you're fucking fault I'm like this." I remembered the things I had witnessed my mother do. "Remember that time you fucked the landlord for the rent money? You did him and he came out of the room drunk and tried to lay with me….You remember that?" I remembered his stank, beer laden breath in my face when my eyes popped open. "Shhh…" he said but I screamed, running from the room, only to meet my Mama at the door. "Girl what's wrong with you." He came out scared, grabbing his clothes and limping from me kicking him in the dick for blocking my way. "You remember what you told me when he left?" She probably wouldn't, but it took me two years of counseling to get over what she told me. "I could have got my damn rent paid up through Christmas if you would have let him take a little dip…damn girl you're so fucking bougie." That was back when she smoked skinny Virginia Slims. She smoked the damn thing hard like a joint and blew the smoke in my face. That's when I figured out that using my pussy to get what I wanted wasn't just acceptable, it was expected. A year later, I was pregnant with the twins. Some guy from the neighborhood that promised riches and ghetto dreams up until I told him I was pregnant. He disappeared without a trace, then his body was found in the river with his face blown off. I felt like my life had ended. Fifteen with two babies and my Mama didn't make my life any easier. Busting into my bedroom one morning yelling at me to get up. "Look, you done had them babies. You gotta get yo ass up and get a job." "But mama what about school?" "Fuck that school shit. If you can't do that and hold down a job then you better sell some ass or something." I didn't sell myself but I knew I had to get the hell out of my mother's house. I did what I had to survive through that. And when mother got saved when I was eighteen, I left the girls with her while I went out of state and worked. I sent money back and did all I could for those girls. I didn't want them growing up like me and I realized that shit happened while they lived with my mother, but I'm sure they never woke up with a half drunk man in their bed. As I rode to the lawyer's office I thought about all of that. How I did some things just to get the bills paid while they grew up and for that little bitch to go behind my back and fuck my husband. The thought hurt me at first, it tore my heart into a million pieces. But nothing hurt my heart worse than my mother telling me to fuck the landlord at fourteen for free rent. That broke my heart, everything after that was child's play. "It's okay Mama...you warned me about her. You told me that she would be my problem child." It was true that's what Mama always told me but what would make my daughter turn on me. "Mrs. Hollins...are you okay?" I snapped out of my day dream back to the lawyer's office. "Yes...sorry. Just my thoughts getting away from me." "Well, I just wanted to let you know we were able to get a larger settlement on your mother's home. It looks like you and your daughters will get three hundred and forty two thousand instead of the amount I told you before." My mind started to swim. "What? Say that again." He repeated himself word for word. "We will have to subtract the loans you have taken against your portion, but that still leaves you with a very substantial amount." I tried to stand but my knees shook, my head started to pound. "Are you okay…?" I heard him say it but I couldn't move my mouth to tell him no. Everything started to spin until there was nothing but darkness. "Ms. Hollins...Ms.

Hollins?" I heard someone calling my name but all of it felt so far away. I tried fighting through the clouds at this bright shining light. "Ms. Hollins, Ms. Hollins?" The more they called my name, the faster I ran until the light was so bright and eventually I began to see again. "There you are. Are you okay?" Mr. Albitol was right in front of me with a few other faces I didn't know. "Yes...I'm fine. What happened?" Sitting up I noticed I was on the floor. Not in chair, not on a couch but my ass was flat on the floor. "You passed out. I think it was the good news that I told you." He laughed, but I was terrified. Passing out wasn't normal, no matter how much money I was supposed to get. "Lord. I'm so embarrassed." Getting up slowly, I felt like the whole staff was packed into the little office. "How long was I out?" "Maybe about a minute or two. Wasn't even long enough for us to call an ambulance." "I am so sorry Mr. Albitol. I am so embarrassed." I wished I could have run out of the office, but my legs still felt like putty. "Is there anyone for you to call?" I tried to think fast but Clarence was out of town again. Even if he was in town, he wouldn't be a viable option. I didn't want to see

Donesha; since the new year I hadn't even laid eyes on her. Just text messages and faking being busy made it easy for us to stay out of each other's way. Little bitch was probably feeling guilty so she stayed out of my way. My mind went into that situation and before I knew, it Mr. Albitol was calling me back. "You sure you are okay, Yvette?" I wasn't sure how to answer that. Mama used to have dizzy spells, then she found out it was heart failure. Am I getting sick? Maybe it was time for me to see a cardiologist and make sure I wasn't at risk for anything hereditary. I put it off so long and now here I was passing out in my lawyer's office. "Is there no one we can call to pick you up?" Mr. Albitol asked and I could only think of one person. The only other man I could trust. "Yeah I have someone. But tell me. When can I get the money?" "All you have to do is sign these papers and we can have the accounts all set up for you and your girls." It was that easy. "Fine. Let's do that now and I'll make a call for my ride," I told him. "Get Mrs. Hollins the papers please," he said to a member of his staff. They went running the instant he gave the orders, and putting the phone to my ear I prayed that he would answer. Sure enough, on the third ring I heard his voice. "Hello…" "Tron, its Yvette. I need your help." He was the only person I could call right now.

Chapter Twenty Four
TRON

I fucked her this morning and now here we were still together this afternoon doing what she wanted. Was I her fucking stool pigeon or something? She had my nuts in a vice, whether it was for sex or for an errand, when Yvette called I had to go running...at least for now. But today we drove in silence. She hadn't said a word since she got in the car. She was gazing out the window as if I wasn't even here. When we finally were within blocks of the house she blurted out questions. "How is my daughter?" Yvette asked. "Getting big. She's almost six months now." "God it's been that long." "Yeah we're almost at June." "Jeez..." She shook her head as I pulled into her driveway. "Has she said anything about me or does she know anything about this?" she asked pointing from me to her and back again. "Naw, she's just been focused on school and the baby's room. She said she just didn't want any negativity in the new year so she doesn't want to see you." For some reason that gave Yvette a hysterical laugh. "She doesn't want the negativity of me? That's hilarious." She laughed as I pulled into her driveway. "Isn't that a bitch?" "What?" She jumped from the car going to the porch like her ass was on fire. "God dammit…" On the porch she walked back and forth cursing and stomping like a toddler. "What the hell is it?" I yelled, getting out of the car. "My chairs. They're gone. Someone is fucking with my porch again." She stomped around then she staggered a bit. "Whoa…" I caught her, grabbing her before she fell. "You have to take it easy," I told her, but there was no calming Yvette down. "Fuck that. I got the cameras now. I'm going to see who the hell this is." She staggered into the house, flopping down on the sofa. "Are you okay." "Why?" "You look flushed." "Yeah I'm great. Actually never been better," she said, her eyes in her phone. I watched her, how she seemed tired her eyes drooping as she tried working through the app. "You seemed tired earlier today too." "You trying to say you didn't have a good time with me?" she asked as I frantically shook my head. "No, that's not what I mean I was just saying that…" "Oh my fucking God." "What?" "That bitch. I should have known it had something to do with his lying ass." She flipped the screen of the phone over so I could see. "What the hell is that?" I asked. "Clarence's ex-wife." "Ex-wife? What the fuck is she doing here?" "I don't know, but I'm done. I'm done with his ass." "You're kicking him out?" "Yeah I've had it with his shit. The cheating bastard fucking my…" She stopped herself. "Fucking with my life. I'm just done. Plus I got good news today," she said standing up slowly. "What's that then?" "I'm getting the inheritance. I'm going to tell the girls soon and they'll know." "Oh yeah…" "And guess what, I'm getting back way more than I thought we were." That sent my mind dancing. I needed money. I was about to be a father and had bills to pay off. I barely scraped by and paid Donesha's tuition payment. "So you're going to tell them soon?" "When everything is finalized I will," she said, walking towards the stairs. "Where are you going now?" "To pack my husband's shit. You should leave. Thanks for giving me a ride home." She seemed different right now, more focused and almost angry. "You sure you're okay?" "Hell yeah, I'm fine. I just have shit to do. Life isn't getting any slower and I'm not getting any younger. Time to get this trash out of my way," she said taking to the stairs. I watched her as she climbed up the steps and disappeared at the top. Just to think, earlier today we were fucking and now she was about to get rid of her husband and she just told me that my girl was going to get three hundred thousand dollars. "Alright I'm gone then…" "Thanks. Lock the bottom lock when you leave." That was it. I was outside, headed towards my car. I counted bills in my head as I drove. Leaving Yvette's house behind I tried to think of everything I had to pay when I got a call. "Hello?" "So you dodging me now?" The number was unfamiliar but I would know the voice anywhere. "Oh wassup Melo?" "You heard my question or you just going to play like you didn't hear?" "Naw man I'm not dodging you." "It feels like it nigga. Where is my payment?" I thought quick, trying to find a good excuse. "Ummm man…" "Umm my ass. Time is up nigga." Melo didn't scream or raise his voice. It was more like a promise and less like a threat but all the same, I heard a click and then a long silence. "What? What does that mean?" The line was dead, I might as well have been talking to myself. "FUCK!" I punched the steering wheel. Waiting at a red light I thought about calling him back. Maybe I could explain or get him some money for the moment until all this inheritance shit became clear. Looking at my phone, I debated on calling him back when I heard screeching tires. I couldn't turn around fast enough to see before the flash of a black car came speeding right up beside me. I couldn't move or react when I saw the gun pointing out the window. All I had time to do was close my eyes. I heard the sound of the windows breaking and my skin felt like it was on fire.

Chapter Twenty Five

DONESHA

"So what brings you in today?" Same me but new therapist all these years later. I would have been fine if it wasn't for Clarence. Now I was a few months removed from that day and I still couldn't stop thinking about it. "I'm having nightmares. I'm really afraid of someone." "Oh...do tell." She took out a notepad scribbling notes as I spilled all of my secrets. I breezed through everything letting it out like some long run on sentence. "Wow..." she said as I finally finished. Readjusting her bun and cleaning her glasses, I could tell she was stalling for time to put everything together. "I have a complicated life." It was the truth, there was nothing simple about me. Everything relationship that I had was strained in some sort of way. "Yeah it is. Do you feel that this man will harm you? You say his name is Clarence." I had no idea, thinking about that day scared me and all I could do was shrug it off to keep from crying. "So you aren't afraid?" "Oh I am. But what can I do about it?" She couldn't answer because there was no answer to this craziness. I had gotten myself into this I was going to have to figure a way out. "I want to say if you do feel like you are in danger, maybe it would be a good time to talk to your mother." I wanted to slap her for even suggesting that. "What would that do?" "Coming clean to her and letting her know about the threat will give you an ally to help and..." "I told you, he said he hits her too. What the hell is she going to do?" She took a deep breath sitting back in her own chair. "I'm sorry I misspoke. I forgot about that part." She shook her head for a moment then sat in silence. "It's just going to be messed up either way. But I'll get through it. Thanks for your time." This wasn't like when I was in undergrad. Back then I thought molestation and abandonment were the worst things that could happen to you, but I was wrong. Being pregnant and your mother's abusive husband potentially being the father is by far the worst thing. I stood to leave, making it to the door before she could say a word. I stopped listening anyway as she called my name a few times to come back. I was halfway to my car about to break down in tears as I waddled my pregnant self to the parking lot when my phone began to ring. "Yeah." I assumed it was the therapist begging me to come back but instead a man's voice filled the phone. "Hello. May I speak to Donesha Hill please?" "Speaking." "This is Sergeant Craters from the Metropolitan police department." My heart stopped beating as I thought about what could of been wrong or what I did wrong. "Yes." "There was an accident involving Trontavious Carter. We need you down to the hospital right away." "Are you serious?" "Yes ma'am. Very serious. How quickly can you be here?" Five minutes ago I was trying to figure out my life and now everything in my life stood still. I didn't know whether to cry or to breakdown, but I needed help. "I'll be right there." With shaking hands I hung up the phone and out of instinct I dialed her number, my hands were working on their own as the phone began to ring. I don't know if it's been guilt or shame that's made me unable to face her, but right now I needed her. "Hello…" "Mom…" The tears came before I could get it out. "Tron's been in an accident. I'm at the school and I need to get to him. I'm so nervous I can't drive." "I'm on my way," was all that she said. No questions, no excuses, she was just on her way. God forgive me for what I've done. I asked the stars as I rubbed my belly. Please don't let this be Clarence's baby. If it was I would never be able to forgive myself and neither would my mother.

Chapter Twenty Six

EVE

Dressed in black from the top of her hoodie to the bottom of her sneakers Eve was good at blending in and going unnoticed. In the dark of night, she was able to get to the side of the house admiring the beauty of the huge home that her baby daddy shared with his woman. "So this is the house that you bought for her?" Eve asked the air, because no one was around to answer. The house looked huge from the outside, a two car garage, two stories as far as she could see with a huge backyard. "Our daughter could have played in that yard," she said while making her way to the backyard. Peeking through the patio window she didn't see anyone home but what she did see made her head pound. "A fucking marble countertop. Glass chandelier, a huge granite top kitchen table." She ogled over all of the details of the house. And the more she saw the more pissed off she became with the man she spent a couple of years serving as his on call sex partner. "You tell me that you love me. Then you buy this bitch a house." Two large plastic trash containers sat on the porch with trash overflowing from it. "What do we have here? Evidence of how horrible of a father you are? How you neglected me and your daughter when we needed you most?" Armed with latex gloves and a flashlight Eve looked through the trash, picking through bags like a dirty raccoon. She didn't see anything of interest, just food wrappers and discarded papers, until she saw it. An order form for invitations. "What is this you planning a little party without your baby's mother?" she asked, but unfolding the order form she had to read it a good five times before it set in. "You are cordially invited to the gender reveal of our child!" Eve screamed the words shrieking in the backyard like a wounded animal. "You piece of shit. You have a baby with her, a gender reveal, and a few months ago you let my daughter die?" Eve was beyond upset as she kicked the trash cans over, spewing the contents all over the back patio. With the swiftness of a martial artist, she produced a can of lighter fluid and matches from her pocket. Dousing the porch in the flammable liquid she made sure to soak the wood particularly heavily near the house. "You built this castle, this life, now how is it going to feel to see it all go up in flames?" She lit the match, instantly sending the patio up in a huge ball of flames. Jumping from the porch, she laughed as the flames took over the wooden structure she had just been standing on. And just like she planned, the fire reached the house, sending the patio window into flames before the loud thunderous sound of glass breaking from the heat made her jump. "Oohhhh fireworks." She clapped as she watched the show. Within two minutes the entire back half of the house was engulfed and finally, she felt a bit of peace. "See if you can put your life back together now." Slipping off her gloves, with her hood up Eve jumped a few fences, taking a more scenic route through the neighbors' backyards as she heard the sound of sirens and fire trucks. By the time she made it back to the street at the end of the block, she could see the entire house was burning. The roof liked like a roasting barbecue pit of flames and she couldn't have been happier. "I'm not done yet you son of a bitch," she told the wind, pretending it was Tron. "I'm just getting started."

To Be Continued…

SNEAK PEEK AT

SCANDALOUS

2

Billie Dureya Shell

Chapter One

BRYAN

Holidays were his busiest time of year and he loved every minute of it. Even now, cleaning up his 'workspace,' as he liked to call it, of any blood was more like a scavenger hunt than real work. Dressed in all black from his black skull cap and gloves all the way down to his black boots, the man was on a mission to finish his job with the precision and care that he was known for. In the pitch dark room he shined the black light across the floor looking for any blood or bodily fluids. "Come on...I know something is out there," he grumbled. Finally, in the corner by the door, he found it - one single drop of blood. Spraying a bleach solution he cleaned the lone piece of evidence and turned the lights back on. Stuffing the tools of his trade back into a black satchel bag that hung off his shoulder, he looked over his work. His target sat slumped over her desk, a mid-forties, blonde-haired marketing executive now dead from two gunshot wounds to the head. It was his best work, but she did put up a bit of a fight, hence the need to check the 'workspace' for any blood particles. He made sure to open a window, letting in the cold air and letting out the full stench of evacuated bodily fluids from his latest kill. "Alright. Looks like I'm all clear," he whispered to himself, shutting off the light again and walking briskly out the office door. Down the hallway and to the steps the athletically built man - tall enough to be a star basketball player - seemed to zoom down the ten flights to the first floor. At the bottom, he calmed himself, steadied his breathing, and just as he was about to go outside his phone rang. "Shit…" He jumped slightly, startled by the phone but the name on the screen wouldn't allow him to ignore it. Family first was always the motto so he answered the phone and entered the cold darkness of night. "Hey Clarence...wassup bruh? Where you at? Sounds noisy," Bryan observed as he entered a dark alley towards a busy street where he could get lost in a crowd. Just before he made it to the road, he carefully took out the weapon he'd used tonight and threw it in a sewer grate. He was almost thankful for the cold; gloved hands eliminated fingerprints but they were more suspicious in warm weather. "I'm in an airport. One last trip before the end of the year...you know the hustle doesn't stop." Clarence laughed and so did Bryan "You're preaching to the choir, fam. I'm on the job right now." "Bryan my brother always working and getting his paper. I'm proud of you bruh." They talked to each other like close brothers but they were more like brothers from a different mother. Step siblings from a relationship that hadn't lasted, the men still called each other brother, especially when one of them needed something. "Oh...just working. You know how that goes." Bryan downplayed the situation as he walked through the streets, blending in with the rest of the holiday shoppers in the downtown shopping district. Everyone was so busy getting out of the cold that no one noticed the man dressed in black from head to toe walking through the crowd. He slipped anonymously through the crowd, all of them oblivious to the fact that he had a gun big enough to kill an elephant on his right hip. "Yeah I feel you bruh. You coming over for our New Year's celebration?" Clarence asked. Bryan thought about it as he made it to his all Black CLS Benz, parked a comfortable seven blocks from his target. "Umm...I don't know about that." Bryan surveyed his surroundings making sure he wasn't followed before jumping in the fine German engineering and taking off. "Come on bruh I need a favor from you." "A favor?" "Is this line secure?" Clarence asked before he continued. "Negative...I will need a second line for that. You know that number." Before Bryan could get the sentence out, his second phone began to ring from the cup holder. "Yeah?" he answered "This is secure right?" Clarence asked urgently. "Yep...wassup." "I got a dilemma I need you to handle." "Like what?" Bryan was down for anything from kidnapping to outright murder; he was what some would call a hit man but he preferred being called a problem solver. "I need you to take care of something for me but… it's a little different. You remember my daughter-in law- right?" Bryan thought quickly as he started the car and slowly left the curb. "Which one?" "The younger one…" Bryan had a damn near photographic memory, he could remember anything and could immediately picture the woman in question. "Lanesha, right?" "Yeah that's the one. I need you to…befriend her and get something back for me." "Ahh, like that one chick in college you had me 'befriend' so you could get a better grade." Clarence laughed at that. Sometimes he forgot about all of their dealings together, some vanilla and some much worse. "Yeah something like that. And she's going to be at the party so…" "Say no more," Bryan answered. "Send me a picture and her info. I'll figure it out." "Aww thanks, bruh. I really appreciate it." "What is this about anyway?" Bryan asked, relaxing a little as he left the shopping district far behind him, along with the skyscraper where his latest victim was slumped over a desk. She wouldn't probably be found until morning and by then he would be so far removed from the area, no one would know where to start with clues. "I got caught up fam..." Clarence hedged. "Be specific." Bryan asked as he shot onto the highway. Merging onto the three lane expressway then shooting past cars like a slingshot in his all black, luxury getaway car. Clarence explained the situation and Bryan listened, filing information into his mind like the human filing cabinet that he was. "So I need you to get close to her. See if you can calm this situation down and maybe if she has companionship then… "Then she won't blow the whistle on you," Bryan said connecting the dots. "Exactly!" Giving his head a small rub he made a quick decision. "Fine...I'll be there." "My brother...thanks fam." "This should square us up on that one situation right?" Bryan hated owing people and he paid back all of his debts but the one he owed his step-brother Clarence was one of his biggest. "Yep, this will make us completely square. You keep her quiet and I'm good." "No dirt naps?" "Nooo...no...not yet at least." Clarence laughed but Bryan found nothing funny. He was completely serious. Killing someone wasn't a laughing matter to Bryan, but he didn't say a word. Instead he just drove, listening to his brother babble for a few minutes. "Alright bruh so I'll see you at my house on New Year's Eve." Clarence finally wound down his steady rant. "Yeah...I'll be there," Bryan said, giving his word and his word was his bond. Rubbing his stubbled chin he thought about what it would take to seduce a woman. He pictured Lanesha, the way she looked the last time he saw her, and he already knew what he had to do. "Alright. See you soon bruh." He had about a week to get ready for his seduction and as he hung up the phone Bryan was already thinking about what he would say. He was the consummate professional and he was unwilling to leave any job to chance, especially when on the job for his family. He would take this just as seriously as a murder-for-hire gig and that meant extensive preparation. Steering with his left hand he used his right to type Lanesha's name into his phone. Using a special database her address, phone number, and recent social media pictures came up. He now had intel on his latest job, and with that information he was sure to have perfect aim and not miss his target.

Chapter Two
YVETTE

A s we lay on the living room floor, me smoking a cigarette and Tron staring at the ceiling, I tried to understand why my daughter would give up all of this for old ass Clarence. Clarence whose signature sex move was getting on top every once in a while. But what I saw him doing on that video wasn't the Clarence I knew. He doesn't do shit like that for me. I cried at first and then I got jealous, hate rising up in me til it was in my brain sending me signals to do something. Now, here I was, resting from the aftermath of my decision. "I guess I should get these cameras down...I gotta get out of here," Tron said as he got up. "What's the rush?" I sat up, watching him fumble to get dressed. "I still got some work to do...and Clarence...Donesha... fuck!" He jumped up as if he had just now realized what we were doing. "I can't believe I did this shit." Shit? My pussy was far from shit, it was gold wrapped in a small package. "But you liked it right?" I asked. He didn't speak at first, instead searching for his jeans, pulling them up over his stained boxers. A DNA test would confirm that my pussy juices and his cum were mixed in to form a beautiful artistic pattern of cum stains on his boxers. "Did you hear me?" "Huh?" "You liked right?" I repeated. He thought for a moment, a small smile starting to crease his lips before he started to shake his head. "Don't shake it off, just admit that you liked this pussy." "Yeah it was good but I'm engaged to your daughter. You're married. We shouldn't have done this." He found his shoes and I watched as he finished getting dressed. Then he found the small stepladder and used it to take down the cameras that were inside the house. It seemed to only take him seconds but when he was done he stood by the door like a little puppy waiting for orders. "Are you leaving?" I asked, disappointed. "Yeah I need to go. But I think we need to figure out right now what this is." I went to him, my naked body fully exposed as I pinned him to the wall. "This is whatever the fuck we want it to be." My lips on his and he didn't move away when I put my hands back into his jeans. "This is my dick now. So when I call...you better come running. Understood?" He stared at me, checking my seriousness but there were no smiles or laughs on my face. This was real life and now that I've let him get a taste he belonged to me, no matter who was in the way. "I hear you but, Yvette, we can't do this. This one time was a mistake and..." He kept going but his lips looked so succulent and pink and all I could see was the look he'd had in his eyes as I pushed his face down between my legs. Now he was standing here talking to me with these lips that had my pussy juices glazed all over them only an hour ago. There was no way he would take that away from me no matter what he said. He belonged to me or else. "You get that...or I'll have to let my daughter see what happened here today," I threatened. "What?" It wasn't hard to bring up the footage of our sexcapade up on the security app. I watched as he held on to my phone speechless, his head shaking more with every position that we moved in until I pulled my phone away from his grasp. "Now this is how we are going to play this. I will call you...and you come running when I say. Got it?" It was a take it or leave it proposition and he had no choice. "Fine...whatever...I just can't believe this shit," he said, rubbing his temples like he was trying to push a migraine away. I wanted to tell him how much I enjoyed my time, and how we could make beautiful love together but my phone rang, stealing the moment. My husband's name appeared across the screen and sucked the joy out of the room. "I have to go..." Tron didn't wait for my permission. He was out the door, running to his car like a ghost was chasing him. "Hello..." I answered the phone with a smile on my face. "Baby I'm sorry for what I did," Clarence blurted out as soon as he heard my voice. I listened to him beg and plead through the phone about how he didn't mean it but was he apologizing for hitting me or fucking my daughter? "I don't know what came over me. Maybe I need to go back to counseling or something...I'm so sorry," he went on. I didn't say a word, just holding the phone listening to his sorry excuses. I wondered how long he and Donehsha had been going on. I thought about all the possible signs and I saw nothing. They hated each other. But now I knew that was an act, nothing was true and everyone in my life was fake. My daughter betrayed me and my husband helped her do it. "Baby do you hear me?" I snapped out of my trance to see that Tron's car was gone and Clarence was still on my line babbling. "Yes I hear you, Clarence. I'm getting tired I need to get some rest." "I'll be home tomorrow, beautiful. Maybe we can talk then." I could have left him now, gotten a divorce and submitted the video of him cheating on me as evidence but I wouldn't get my full pay out. Per the prenuptial agreement I would get almost nothing, even if he cheated. Just a little while longer...play the game for a little while, I told myself. I had a plan but it wasn't for the weak and I could play this game better than anybody. "I love you Yvette and I'm sorry..." "I know you do baby. It's okay..." "Really?" I wanted to laugh at his excitement. Hell no it wasn't okay that he hit me but I let him think it was. "Maybe when I get back we can try for a baby one last time." I wanted to laugh at that too. Clarence always wanted to talk about kids. Even though my uterus was closed and would probably be going through menopause soon, I said whatever I could to keep him at ease. No use in spoiling my big reveal before everything was in place. "Yeah maybe we can try one last time this year," I cooed. For a man that was fucking my daughter you would think he would want as little to do with me as possible, but here he was begging me to have a baby. I wonder what he's telling Donesha. "You have no idea how good it feels to hear you say that. I love you baby. I'm all yours for the holidays all the way through the new year." I rolled my eyes at that. I didn't want to be around him non-stop. He had no idea how good it felt to fuck a real man half my age and now I was addicted. But the more my husband thought we were on good terms, the better. Revenge is best served cold anyways.

EVE

Every hall, floor, nook, and cranny of Homer Seales Regional Hospital was engraved in Eve's brain. She had walked the halls throughout each night for the past few weeks, to move around and clear her mind. Anything to take her mind off her tiny infant who was fighting for her life. Taking the elevator up to the NICU, Eve went about her normal routine. Smiling and saying hi to all the other parents and nurses that were crowded outside the sterilized room. They all seemed to stare at her and Eve pretended not to notice, but everyone knew that today was the last day. Her angel was going home. She hung up her belongings and began the fifteen minute procedure of scrubbing every particle of dirt and bacteria from her hands. An aid appeared, helping her put on scrubs, head cap, and a mask. Soon she looked like a hazmat worker, covered in yellow with white latex gloves on her hands. "You ready?" the woman asked, but Eve would never be ready for what she had to do. Instead of crying and prolonging the inevitable she simply nodded her head, unable to talk for fear the tears would start flowing. The sounds of machines buzzing and the faint swoosh of ventilators was the soundtrack of the NICU. Eve stepped slowly over to the miniature heated dome that was what her daughter had known as home since the premature delivery. Usually the tiny dome would be dark, filled with tubes, tape, and gauze. But today the lights were on and her little baby was no longer attached to machines but instead dressed and peaceful in a small pink dress. No more cords, tubes, or ventilators were in the way, just a tiny baby with her eyes closed, like a small princess taken away before she could begin. "She looks like she's just sleeping," Eve said from behind her hospital issued mask. Six weeks and her baby girl fought a good fight but now she was resting for eternity with the angels, up in the stars. Today she had finally been called home. "You know her dad didn't come see her...not once." Eve's her voice cracked as she spoke to baby Neveah's nurse. "I named her Neveah because it was Heaven spelled backwards. Now she's in Heaven and he never got to meet her. He didn't come, not even when I told him that this would be happening." Eve wanted to cry, she felt the aching in her eye sockets and intense weight on her chest but no more words would come out. "Yeah she looks peaceful. We got her dressed up for you just like you asked. The priest should be on his way soon," the nurse told her, but there was no need. She just wanted to be alone with her daughter. "Do you want to hold her one last time?" the nurse asked. She wasn't sure if it was healthy to hold her baby's dead body but this would be the only time she would hold the small child without the interference of tubes and machines. "Sure..." Eve sat down in the rocking chair as the nurse placed the peacefully deceased angel in her arms. She had grown a bit since she was born but not enough. There had been too many complications following a risky surgery due to an infection. A week ago the doctors told her there was nothing else they could do. Baby Neveah had fought all she could, but the time was drawing near. "She looks really pretty in this outfit," Eve said as she traced her fingers over the preemie clothes. Neveah was so small that the small outfit sagged on her but it was better than the white hospital issued onesies that she had worn constantly. "I'll leave you alone with her." The nurse left the pair alone as Eve rocked the small baby back and forth. She searched the infant's face for features that were like her own but she couldn't find one. It was as if she hadn't even given birth to the child. From the top of her little head to the bottom of her feet she saw nothing but Tron. "It's okay baby. He'll figure out one day that he missed out on something special with you." She kissed the small cheek. Where she used to feel warmth was now turning colder and heavier by the second. Her baby was gone, she knew that now. The time passed and, although it had felt like only minutes to Eve as she rocked the baby back and forth, several hours went by before the nurses came to intervene. "It's time now, Eve. We need to take her now," they said. Taking her meant putting her in the morgue. They tried not to say those words but Eve knew what they meant. "But I don't want her to go....I can't believe she's gone." "Do you know what arrangements you will make yet?" asked a nurse, kindly. With so little money, her only option was cremation. That was another thing that pained her soul, to have her little princess burned and ground to dust because her father didn't care enough to send money for a proper burial. "I'll have her cremated and from there...I'm not sure," she admitted as she placed her baby girl down in the plastic crib. She said her goodbyes, giving her a kiss on the cheek. The nurse gave her a hug, a long embrace after spending six weeks together talking, crying, and laughing. Caring for Neveah had created a small bond between the two women. They let go of each other and without a word Eve left, trying to leave the hospital without breaking down on the way to her car. She took off her scrubs in a daze, throwing it all away in trash cans as she left. There was no one waiting to take her home like in the movies.

There was no long line of people coming with her to talk out her situation. Instead she walked to her car alone, thinking of all the things she had done wrong in her pregnancy. Partying into her eighth week when she realized she hadn't seen her period. A haphazard home pregnancy test that she stole from the dollar store gave her two blue lines instead of one. A clue that she was pregnant, but how could she have a baby? Eve was barely twenty-one, with no money, living in a studio apartment, struggling to pay rent. But sure enough, a trip to the clinic confirmed that she was one hundred percent with child. Telling Tron was okay at first. He seemed excited, taking her to dinner and going away for a nice weekend. But the next week she couldn't reach him and when she did, he said one sentence that crushed her soul. "I think you should get an abortion." The A word hadn't even crossed Eve's mind until he said it. When she refused he went into a rage, telling her that he would never be there and she would raise the baby on her own. "How am I supposed to tell my gal about this?" she heard him mutter when he thought she wasn't listening. She was so busy crying that she never told him that she heard those words, she never had a chance to make him apologize. He hung up that day and refused to take her calls. Tracking him down at work was the only way to put a stop to her endless worry. But when she finally saw him the unthinkable happened. She went into early labor brought on by the undue stress. Now she was getting into her cold car, her hands still smelling of the hospital antiseptic and almost numb as she tried to start her car. Everything was numb from her brain down to her feet so she barely could feel the gas pedal as she drove out of the parking lot. As she drove, she kept taking a long sniff of her hands, bathing her senses in the smell that reminded her of her firstborn. That smell would forever sit in her memory, linking her to a daughter that would never come home. That thought was stuck in her brain and now, in the comfort of her car, the thoughts finally became too much. She cried, the tears coming down as she held her stomach, where her baby should still have been. She wasn't due for another two months - a lot of time for a baby to grow and mature to be ready for the world. "I'm sorry I robbed you of that...I'm sorry that I was thinking about him and not about you," she sobbed, barely able to get the words out through her tears. From the hospital parking lot all the way to her house she cried and cried, endless tears that seemed to get worse and worse. Inside she checked into what was more like a jail than a studio apartment. All around were the reminders that she was supposed to be a mother. A crib sat in the corner and various baby clothes were there as well. Lying in bed she cried and cried with no one to console her and tell her it would be alright. She cried until she got sick. She cried herself to sleep and when she woke up she cried some more. Alone in her apartment with the shades drawn, she tried to find herself or at least figure out where she made the wrong turn. Every time she tried to track the problem she always ended up back in the same place. "Tron...it's all your fucking fault." She stared at the picture of them both that sat on her nightstand. The picture from one of their dates, basking in each other's company and seeming so deep in love. Little did she know it was all a show, a lie, and she was the side chick being used by a classic manipulator. "You lied to me... you told me that you loved me and you cared about me then...then you deserted me," she told the picture but it was stuck in time. Stuck back in the time when she knew nothing about the real Trontavious. "But you lied to not just me...you lied to us." She threw the picture and it landed perfectly in the middle of the dozen or so mementos scattered across her bed. Photos, documents, reports, and a DNA test request lay across her bed painting a picture of the man she had called her lover - Mr. Trontavious Carter. "I hate you...I fucking hate you!!" she screamed at his photographed face, but that didn't do her anger justice. She had vowed not to do this but after being ignored she had no choice. She leaped up to her feet and went in search of her phone. With the sun just now setting, Eve grabbed her phone and dialed the number she had memorized. "Hello, Auto Sales, this is Jessica..." "Yes I need to speak with Trontavious Carter, please." The phone went silent, no clicks, rings, or a request to hold on. Instead there was nothing but awkward silence on the line. "Hello?" Eve looked at the receiver making sure the call hadn't dropped. "Hello…" "Yes…yes ma'am," the receptionist's responded, her move to unmute the line was way more obvious than she tried to make it and pushing Eve further to the end of irritation. "May I ask who's calling?" "Why?" Eve snapped back at her, more annoyed by the second. "Can't you just put me through?" Why does it matter who it is? "Umm…I'm sorry ma'am," the receptionist said robotically, like she was reading from a script. "Trontavious no longer works here." The wheels in Eve's head started turning. He told her to say this. He is avoiding me, she told herself as her anger began to rise. "What do you mean? He was working there a month ago…now all of a sudden poof…he's gone?" She looked at the phone as if she were being tricked in some way. "Put Tron on the phone, bitch," he growled into the receiver, wishing she could jump through the phone and strangle the receptionist with her bare hands. "Excuse me ma'am…Don't curse at me." Thoughts of her lost child tumbled around in her head and in an instant Eve's temper exploded through her mouth and into the phone. "PUT TRON ON THE PHONE, BITCH!" she screamed but before she was done pronouncing the last syllable the phone went dead. "FUCK!" Throwing the phone on the bed she balled her fist up and sent it through the wall. Plaster and drywall dust covered her arm as she screamed, wishing that the hole was in Tron's head instead of in her bedroom wall. "He's there. He just doesn't want to talk to you," she reasoned with herself, but that line of reasoning was unacceptable. "No...no...no... that's still not a reason," she told herself back. She needed him to understand that this wasn't right. "Regardless of that, he still missed her birth. He missed everything. Now she's gone and he never even knew her name!" She began to cry, seeing flashes of the life she had planned go up in smoke then reappear as her dead daughter dressed in pink. The shaking and crying made her knees buckle as she sobbed, crying out for help. Eventually the tears dried and the choking stopped and Eve was left holding her legs and rocking back and forth with a focused gaze on the nightstand picture. After a while the picture became real to her. He wasn't in an inanimate frame but was an actual person held in time inside her bedroom. With the same smile and expression, he stood in front of her with a cheesy grin. "After all you've put me through. You're just going to smile?" she asked the hologram Tron that was now growing bigger in her space. "You know what Tron… I'm going to make you wish that you never met me. That you had never been born. And I'm going to make you regret missing my child's life. With everything in me I will make you suffer you sonofabitch!" Eve yelled, jumping to her feet. In her reality she was grabbing Tron by the throat, squeezing it until the smile faded away but what she was really holding was the broken picture frame with broken glass cutting through her hand. A crunched picture of Tron was in the middle of the mess, covered in Eve's own blood as the glass ripped through her soft skin. She wanted to scream from the pain, from the sight of her own flesh being torn apart by Tron but the screams wouldn't leave her mouth. In fact, her lips wouldn't even part. Instead she walked calmly to the bathroom. Grabbing peroxide, bandages, and tweezers she removed the bits of glass with the precision of a surgeon, one by one without making a sound. The picture of Tron was now scratched and stained with blood and Eve had no intention of changing that. She didn't even bother to wash off the blood. "That's how your ass deserves to be. Covered in blood you bitch…" She coughed and spit a perfect glob of her saliva onto the picture. Looking in the mirror, the bags under her eyes, messy bun, and scraggly eyebrows meant nothing. She had a calling now, something she had to do. It was clear in her spirit that Tron needed to be taught a lesson. He had to pay, and the best way to do that was to pour every bit of energy she had into his demise.

New York Times & International Best Selling Author Billie Dureyea Shell was born in Compton California and now lives in Ladera Heights with his wife and kids who he loves to spend time with. He is the Owner of several properties in the Los Angeles area and gives back to his community by providing low income housing to those who need it. He stated "It doesn't matter where you at or where you from it's what you do with your time. There's nothing you can't do if you put your mind to it".

www.ingramcontent.com/pod-product-compliance
Lightning Source LLC
Chambersburg PA
CBHW021139110726
47900CB00002B/421